ROLE OF HONOR

JAMES BOND

ROLE OF HONOR

JOHN GARDNER

PEGASUS BOOKS
NEW YORK

ROLE OF HONOR

Pegasus Books LLC
80 Broad Street, 5th Floor
New York, NY 10004

First Pegasus Books trade paperback edition 2012

Library of Congress Cataloging-in-Publication Data is available.

ISBN: 978-1-60598-339-4

10 9 8 7 6 5 4 3 2 1

Printed in the United States of America
Distributed by W. W. Norton & Company, Inc.
www.pegasusbooks.us

For
Beryl & Gil

Contents

ROLE OF HONOR

– 1 –

Robbery with Violets

THE ROBBERY OF SECURITY VANS can take place at any time of the day, though, as a rule the Metropolitan Police do not encounter hijackers attempting a quick getaway during the rush hour. Nor do they expect trouble with a cargo that is sewn up tight. Only a privileged few knew exactly when the Kruxator Collection would arrive in the country. That it was due to come to Britain was common knowledge, and one had only to read a newspaper to discover that March 15 was the day on which the fabled group of paintings and jewelry was to go on display—for two weeks—at the Victoria and Albert Museum.

The Kruxator Collection is so called after its

founder, the late Niko Kruxator, whose fabulous wealth arose from sources unknown, for he had arrived penniless in the United States—or so he had always said—about the time of the Wall Street Crash in October 1929. By the time he died, in 1977, most people thought of him as the Greek shipping magnate, but he still held his interest in Kruxator Restaurants, and the great international chain of Kruxlux Hotels. He was also sole owner of the Kruxator Collection, which he left to his country of adoption—all three hundred paintings and seven hundred fantastic objets d'art, including three incredible icons dating back to the fifteenth century, smuggled out of Russia at the time of the Revolution, and no fewer than sixteen pieces once owned by the Borgias: a collection certainly beyond price, though insured for billions of dollars.

The two-week London showing of the Kruxator Collection would be the last in its tour of European capitals before the whole consignment was returned to its permanent home in New York, Niko having left an endowment for the building in which these priceless objects could be displayed. Niko Kruxator wanted to be remembered, and he had taken steps to make certain that his name would be permanently linked with those of Van Gogh, Brueghel, El Greco, Matisse, and Picasso. Not that he was knowledgeable about art, but he could sense a fair bargain that would appreciate in value.

A private security firm looked after the precious oils, artifacts and gems on a permanent basis, though host countries were expected to provide extra protection. Nobody was in any doubt that the two armored vans, into which the exhibits fitted, were at constant risk. When the collection was on display, the most elaborate electronics protected each item.

The cargo arrived at Heathrow on an unannounced 747 at six minutes past one in the afternoon. The Boeing was directed to an unloading bay far away from the passenger terminals—near the old Hunting Clan hangars, which still display the name of that company, in large white letters.

The pair of armored vans was waiting, having taken the sea route during the previous night after depositing the collection at the Charles de Gaulle airport in Paris. Two unmarked police cars, each containing four armed plainclothes officers, were now in attendance.

The loaders were trusted employees of the Kruxator Collection itself, who knew their task so well that the entire cargo was off the aircraft and packed into the vans within hours. The unassuming convoy, led by one of the police cars, the other taking up the rear, set off to make a circuit of the perimeter before joining the normal flow of traffic through the underpass and out onto the M4 motorway. It was just after five-fifteen and the light was beginning to go, the traffic starting to build up both in and out of the capital.

Even so, within half an hour the procession arrived at the end of the motorway where the road narrows to two lanes, taking vehicles onto what is dubiously known as the Hammersmith Flyover and then into the Cromwell Road.

Later reports from the police cars—which were in touch by radio with the armored vans—showed a certain amount of confusion during the early part of the journey. An eye-catching black girl, driving a violet-colored sports car, managed to come between the leading car and the first van, just as the convoy climbed the ramp onto the Flyover; while, at the rear, an equally striking white girl, in a violet dress, driving a black sports car, cut between the second van and the police car in the rear.

At first nothing alarming was reported through the radio links, though the separation of police vehicles and armored vans was soon made even greater by the behavior of the two girls who had tucked a Lancia and a Ferrari neatly into the convoy. The trailing police car made two efforts to overtake and get back into position, but the two sports cars either swung out to prevent traffic from getting in or pulled over to allow other private cars, lorries and taxis to overtake. By the time they reached the Cromwell Road not only had the gap between the police and the armored vans widened, but also the two vans had themselves been separated.

The route had been chosen to ensure maximum

14

security. The convoy was to swing left off the Cromwell Road and proceed into Kensington High Street, then turn right before Knightsbridge into the one-way system at Exhibition Road so as to gain access to the rear of the Victoria and Albert Museum, well away from the exposed garden forecourt at the front of the building.

One police car had reached the Royal Garden Hotel, on the High Street side of Kensington Gardens, and the other was only just entering the far end of the High Street, when radio communications abruptly ceased.

The lead car broke all security regulations, activating its klaxon and U-turning across a blocked mass of traffic to make its way back along Kensington High Street. The rear car, also in some panic, began to move forward aggressively. A chaos of honking, hooting vehicles was suddenly smothered in a thick pall of choking, violet-colored smoke. Later, the drivers—and shotgun riders—of the two vans gave identical accounts of what occurred.

"The colored smoke was just there. No warning, no bombs, nothing, just dense colored smoke out of nowhere. Then everything in the cab went alive, as though we'd developed some terrible electrical fault. Naturally, when that happens, you turn off the engine, but the shocks kept coming, and we realized there was danger of being electrocuted. Getting out was a gut reaction . . ."

No one recalled anything after taking off the electronic locks, and all four men were later discovered, still in safety helmets and flak jackets, neatly laid out on the pavement. They were treated—like many others—for respiratory problems, for the smoke had had an unpleasant effect on the lungs.

The two vans simply disappeared, as though someone had opened up the road, dropped them into the hole and then closed it perfectly over them.

The police inspector in charge of the investigation told viewers of *News at Ten* that evening that the robbery had been planned to the second. It must have been rehearsed again and again. So precise was the timing that one might well suppose it to have been a computerized theft. The only clues were the two sports cars and the descriptions of their drivers. The Central Registry, however, soon revealed that the sports car number plates—noted accurately by police officers—had never been issued to any vehicle.

The Kruxator robbery was daring, exact, brilliant and very costly. The lack of progress made by the police investigating it remained in the news for the best part of a month. Even sly comments concerning a breach of security, and the sudden resignation of a senior member of the Secret Intelligence Service—by name Commander James Bond—were lost to the Kruxator headlines, pushed back to a corner of page two and soon altogether out of the public eye.

– 2 –

A Frivolous
and Extravagant Manner

IN THE BEGINNING, Standing Orders were quite clear. Paragraph 12(c) instructed that

> *Any officer, classified as being on active duty, who is subject to any alteration in private financial status will inform Head of A Section, giving full details, and providing any documentation that is thought either necessary or desirable by Head of A.*

A Section is, of course, Accounts, but confidential information—such as James Bond's Australian legacy—automatically went personally to M, Records and the Chief of Staff as well.

In the ordinary commercial world, Bond would naturally have received numerous warm expressions of congratulations on such an unexpected windfall. Not so in the Service. Those who work for Records are tight-lipped by tradition as well as by training. Neither M, Bond's Chief of Service, nor Bill Tanner, M's Chief of Staff, would think of bringing the matter up, for both were of the old school, which, rightly, considered details of private money to be of a personal nature. The fact that they both knew would never stop them pretending they did not. It was, then, almost a shock when M himself mentioned it.

The months before Bond received the news of his legacy had been dull with routine. He always found the office paperwork of his job debilitating and boring, but that summer—now eighteen months ago— was particularly irksome, especially as he had taken all his leave early, a mistake that condemned him to day after day of files, memos, directives and other people's reports. As so often happened in Bond's world there was absolutely nothing—not even a simple confidential courier job—to alleviate the drudgery of those hot months.

Then came the legacy. It arrived, literally out of the blue, in a thick manila envelope with a Sydney postmark, and fell with a heavy plop through his letter box early in the following November. The letter was from a firm of solicitors who for many years had acted for the younger brother of Bond's father, an uncle whom Bond had never seen. Uncle Bruce, it appeared, had died a wealthy man, leaving every penny of his estate to his nephew James, who hitherto had enjoyed a little private money. Now his fortunes were drastically changed.

The whole settlement came to around a quarter of a million sterling. There was one condition to the will. Old Uncle Bruce had a sense of humor and decreed that his nephew should spend at least one hundred thousand pounds within the first four months in "a frivolous and extravagant manner."

Bond did not have to think twice about how he might best comply with such an eccentric proviso. Bentley motor cars had always been a passion, and he had sorely resented getting rid of the old models that he had owned, driven, enjoyed and loved. During the last year he had genuinely lusted after the brand-new Bentley Mulsanne Turbo. When the will was finally through probate, he took himself straight down to Jack Barclay's showrooms, in Berkeley Square, and ordered the hand-built car—in his old favorite British Racing Green, with a magnolia interior.

One month later, he visited the Rolls-Royce Car Division at Crewe, spending a pleasant day with the chief executive and explaining that he wanted no special technology built into the car apart from a small concealed weapon compartment and a long-range telephone, which would be provided by the security experts at CCS. The Mulsanne Turbo was delivered in the late spring, and Bond—having put down the full price with the order—was happy to get rid of the remaining statutory thirty thousand pounds plus by spending it on friends, mainly female, and himself, in a spree of high living such as he had not enjoyed for many years.

But 007 was not so easily brought out of the doldrums. He longed for some kind of action—a craving that he slaked with too many late nights, the excitement of the gaming tables, and a lukewarm affair with a girl he had known for years—a small romance that guttered out like a candle flame after a few months. So even this period of lotus eating failed to remove that unsettled, edgy sense that his life had lost both purpose and direction.

There was one week, in the late spring, when he found some pleasure with the Q Branch Armorer, Major Boothroyd, and his delectable assistant, Q'ute, testing a hand gun the Service was toying with using on a regular basis: the ASP 9mm, an American-made combat modification of the 9mm Smith & Wesson. Bond found it one of the most satisfying hand guns he had ever used.

Then, in the middle of August, when London was crowded with tourists and a torpor hung over the Regent's Park Headquarters, there came a summons from M's secretary, the faithful Miss Moneypenny, and Bond found himself in his chief's office, with Bill Tanner in attendance. It was here, on the ninth floor, overlooking the dry, hot and dusty park, that M surprised him by bringing up the matter of the Australian legacy.

Moneypenny was far from her usual flirtatious self while Bond waited in the outer office, giving him the distinct impression that, whatever the cause of M's summons, the news could not be good. The feeling was heightened once he was allowed into the main office.

Both the Chief of Staff and M looked wary. M's eyes did not even meet Bond's, and Tanner hardly turned to acknowledge his presence.

"We have a pair of Russian ambulance chasers in town," M stated, baldly and without emphasis, once Bond was seated in front of his desk.

"Sir." There was no other possible response to this opening gambit.

"New boys to us," M continued. "No diplomatic cover, French papers, but definitely high-quality ambulance chasers." The Head of Service was talking about Russian operatives whose specific task was to recruit potential informants, agents, traitors.

"You want me to put them on the first aircraft back to Moscow, sir?" Bond's heart rose a little, for even that simple chore would be better than sitting around the office shuffling papers.

M ignored the offer. Instead he looked at the ceiling. "Come into money, 007. That's what I hear."

Bond found himself almost shocked by M's remark. "A small legacy . . ."

M raised his eyebrows, quizzically muttering the word "Small?"

"The ambulance chasers are high-powered professionals." Bill Tanner spoke from the window. "They've both had some success in other parts of the world—Washington, for instance—though there's never been hard evidence. Washington and Bonn. These fellows got in very quietly on both those occasions, and nobody knew about them until it was too late. They did a lot of damage in Washington. Even more in Bonn."

"The orders to expel arrived after the birds had flown," M interjected.

"So, now you know they're here—in the UK—and you want some solid evidence?" An unpleasant thought had crept into Bond's mind.

Bill Tanner came over, dragging a chair so that he could sit close to Bond. "Fact is, we've got wind at an early stage. We presume they imagine we don't know of their presence. Our brothers at 'Five' have been cooperative for once . . ."

"They're here, and active, then." Bond tried to remain calm, for it was not like M or Tanner to beat about the bush. "You want hard evidence?" he asked again.

Tanner took a deep breath, like a man about to unburden his soul. "M wants to mount a dangle," he said quietly.

"Tethered goat. Bait," M growled.

"Me?" Bond slipped a hand into his breast pocket, withdrawing his gunmetal cigarette case, and lit up one of his H. Simmons specials, bought in bulk from the old shop, which still exists in Burlington Arcade.

"Me?" Bond repeated. "The tethered goat?"

"Something like that."

"With respect, sir, that's like talking of a woman being slightly pregnant." He gave a bleak smile. "Either I'm to be the bait, or I'm not."

"Yes," M cleared his throat, plainly embarrassed by what he was about to suggest. "Well . . . it really came to us because of your . . . your little windfall." He stressed the word "little."

"I don't see what that's got to do with it . . ."

"Let me put a couple of questions to you." M fiddled with his pipe. "How many people really know you've, er, come into money?"

"Obviously those with need to know in the Service, sir. Apart from that only my solicitor, my late uncle's solicitor and myself . . ."

"Not reported in any newspapers? Not bandied about? *Not* public knowledge?"

"Certainly not public knowledge, sir."

M and Tanner exchanged quick, knowing glances.

"You have been living at a somewhat extravagant pace, 007," M scowled.

Bond remained silent, waiting. As he had thought, it was not good.

"You see, James," Tanner took up the conversation, "there has been some talk. Gossip. People notice things and the word, around Whitehall, is that Commander Bond is living a shade dangerously—gambling, the new Bentley, er . . . ladies, money changing hands . . ."

"So?" He was not going to make it any easier for them.

"So, even our gallant allies in Grosvenor Square have been over asking questions. They do it when a senior officer suddenly changes his habits."

"The Americans think I'm a security risk?" Bond bridled. "Damned cheek."

"Enough of that, 007," M retorted. "They have every right to ask. You *have* been acting the playboy recently."

"And if they get touchy," Tanner interjected, "then there's no knowing what thoughts are running through the minds of those who watch from Kensington Gardens."

"Rubbish," Bond almost spat. "Those who are not our friends know me too well. They'll ferret out the legacy in no time—if they're interested . . ."

"Oh, they're interested all right," Tanner continued. "You haven't noticed anything?"

Bond's brow creased as he shook his head.

"No? Well, why should you? They've been very discreet. Not a twenty-four-hour surveillance or anything like that, but our people on the street have reported that you're under observation. Odd days, occasional nights, questions in unlikely places."

Bond swore silently. He felt foolish. *Even at home, behave as though you're in the field,* they taught. Elementary, and he had not even noticed.

"Where's this leading, then?" he asked, dreading the answer.

"To the dangle." Tanner gave a half smile. "To a small charade, with you as the central character, James."

Bond nodded. "As I said. I'm going to be the bait."

"It seems reasonable enough." M turned his attention to his pipe. "The situation is ideal . . ."

This time Bond did explode, voicing his feelings with some venom. It was the most stupid ploy he had ever heard of. No recruiting officer from any foreign agency would seriously consider him. And, if they did, their masters would put the blight on it in ten seconds flat.

"You're not really serious about this, are you?"

"Absolutely, 007. I agree, on the face of it they'll steer clear of you; but we have to look at the facts— they *are* more than interested already . . ."

"Never in a thousand years . . ." Bond started again.

"We've already written the scenario, 007, and we're going along with it. Do I have to remind you that you're under discipline?"

There were no options, and Bond, feeling the whole business was sheer madness, could only sit and listen to the litany of the scheme as, between them, M and Tanner outlined the bare bones, like a pair of theatrical directors explaining motivation to a reluctant actor.

"At an appropriate moment we haul you in," M said.

"Enquiry in camera," counterpointed Bill Tanner.

"Making certain the Press are tipped off."

"Questions in the House."

"Hints of scandal. Corruption in the Service."

"And you resign."

"Giving the impression that, in reality, we've cast you into outer darkness. And if that doesn't lure the ambulance chasers, then there's something else in the wind. Wait, and do as I say, 007."

And so it had happened—though not because of the ambulance chasers, as they had told him. Rumors ran along the corridors of power; there was gossip in the clubs, tattle in the men's rooms of government departments, hints to the Press, hints *by* the Press, even questions in the House of Commons, and finally the resignation of Commander James Bond.

– 3 –

Outer Darkness

IN THE MONTH BEFORE the Kruxator robbery, Bond himself had been following a hedonistic routine. He spent days lazing in bed until noon and ventured forth in the evenings, to restaurants, clubs and gaming houses, usually with a pretty girl in tow. The Press, which had hounded him at the moment of his resignation, hardly approached him again. He had no contact at all with his former employers. In fact they went out of their way to avoid him. One evening, he found himself at the Inn on the Park, seated only two tables from Ann Reilly—the attractive and talented assistant to the Armorer in Q Branch. Bond caught her eye and smiled, but she merely looked through him, coldly, as though he did not exist.

Then, toward the end of April, around noon one

mild, bright Thursday, the telephone rang in Bond's flat. Bond, who had been shaving, grabbed at the handset, as though he would like to strangle the trilling tone.

"Yes?" he growled in response.

"Oh!" The voice was female, and surprised. "Is that 58 Dean Street? The Record Shop?"

"It's not 58 anything." Bond did not even smile.

"But I'm sure I dialed 734-8777 . . ."

"Well, you didn't get it." He slammed the receiver down.

Later in the afternoon, however, he telephoned his date—a favorite blonde hostess with British Airways—to cancel their evening. Instead of dinner for two at the Connaught, Bond went, alone, to Veeraswamy's, that most excellent Indian restaurant in Swallow Street, where he ate a chicken vindaloo with all the trimmings, lingered over his coffee, then paid the bill and left on the dot of nine-fifteen. The magnificent uniformed and bearded doorman threw him a quivering salute, then loudly hailed a cab. Bond gave the driver his home address, but when the taxi reached the top of St. James's, he told the driver to pull over, paid him, and set off on foot, to follow what appeared to be an aimless route, turning into the side streets, crossing roads suddenly, doubling back on himself a number of times, loitering at corners, making certain he was not being followed. Eventually, clinging to this patient and devious routine, he ended up in a doorway near St. Martin's Lane.

For two minutes, Bond stood looking up at a lighted window across the road. At precisely ten o'clock the oblong of light turned black, then lit again, went black, lit and stayed on.

Quickly Bond crossed the road, disappearing through another doorway, up a narrow flight of stairs, across a landing and up four more steps to a door that bore the legend RICH PHOTOGRAPHY LTD. MODELS AVAILABLE.

When he pressed the small button to the right of the lintel, the chimes, associated with a well-known brand of cosmetics, ding-donged from far away inside. There were faint footsteps and the click of bolts being drawn.

The door opened to reveal Bill Tanner, who nodded and moved his head in a gesture indicating that Bond should enter. He followed Tanner along a small passage, the paintwork peeling, and a cloying smell of cheap scent hanging in the air, then through the door at the far end. The room was very small and cluttered. A bed with an eye-battering coverlet stood in one corner. A seedy Teddy-Bear lounged on a bright orange, heart-shaped imitation silk nightdress case. A small wardrobe faced the bed, its door half open, displaying a pathetic row of women's clothes, while a tiny dressing table was crammed with bottles and jars of cosmetics. Above a popping gas fire, a print of *The Green Lady* looked down from a plastic frame upon a pair of easy chairs that would not have been out of place in a child's Wendy House.

"Come in, 007. Glad to see you can do simple mathematics." The figure in one of the chairs turned, and Bond found himself looking into M's familiar cold gray eyes.

Tanner closed the door, and now crossed to a table on which were set several bottles and glasses.

"Good to see you, sir," Bond said with a smile, holding out a hand. "Seven and three equals ten. Even I can manage that."

"Nobody in tow?" Bill Tanner asked, sidling toward the window that Bond had viewed from the far side of the street.

"Not unless they've got a team of a hundred or so footpads and about twenty cars on me. Traffic's thick as treacle tonight. Always bad on Thursdays—late night shopping, and all the commuters staying up to meet their wives and girlfriends."

The telephone gave a good old-fashioned ring, and Tanner got to it in two strides.

"Yes," he said, then, again. "Yes. Good. Right." Replacing the receiver he looked up with a smile. "He's clear, sir. All the way."

"I told you—" Bond began, but Tanner cut him short with an invitation to take a gin and tonic with them. Bond scowled, shaking his head. "I've had enough alcohol to float several small ships in the past few weeks . . ."

"So we all noticed," M grunted.

"Your instructions, sir. I could remind you that I said at the outset nothing would come of it. Nobody in our business would even begin to believe I'd left the Service, just like that. The silence has been deafening."

M grunted again, "Sit down, 007. Sit down and listen. The silence has not been so deafening. On the contrary, the isle is full of noises, only you have been on a different frequency. I fear we've led you on a merry dance, but it was necessary for you to remain ignorant of the true object of this operation—that is, until we had established to the various intelligence communities that you were persona non grata as far as we're concerned. Forget what we told you during our last meeting. Now, we have the real target. Look on this picture, and on this, and this."

Like an experienced poker player, M laid out three photographs, one man and two women.

"The man," he said at last, "is presumed dead. His name was Dr. Jay Autem Holy." The finger touched one photograph, then moved on to the next. "This lady is his widow, and this—" the finger prodded toward the third photograph—"this is the same lady. Looks so different that, should her husband come back from the dead, which is in the cards, he would never recognize her."

M picked up the final photograph. "She will give you the details. In fact she'll give you a little training as well."

The woman in question was plump, with mousy brown hair, thick-lensed spectacles, thin lips and a sharp nose too big for the bone structure of her rather chubby face. At least that was how she looked in the photograph taken some years ago when she was married to Jay Autem Holy. M also maintained that Bond would not recognize her now. That did not surprise him when he studied the second photograph.

"You're sending me on another course?" Bond mused rather absently without looking up.

"Something like that. She's waiting for you now."

"Yes?"

"In Monaco. Monte Carlo. Hotel de Paris. Now listen carefully, 007. There's a good deal for you to absorb, and I want you on the road early next week. First, her name is Persephone Proud. Second, you must, naturally, still consider yourself as one cast into outer darkness. But this is what we—together with our American cousins—planned from the start."

M talked earnestly for about fifteen minutes, allowing no interruptions, before Bond was escorted through another elaborate security routine to get him safely clear of the building and on the rest of his way home in a taxi without being followed. Not for the first time, Bond had been given another life, a double identity. But unlike all the many parts he had played for the honor of his country, this was to appear—to all but M and Tanner—as a role of dishonor.

– 4 –

Proud Percy

BOND PARTICULARLY ENJOYED the drive through France, down to the Midi, for it was the first time he had been able to let the huge Mulsanne Turbo off the leash. The car seemed to revel in the business of doing its job with perfection. It pushed its long, elegant snout forward and then, like a thoroughbred in peak condition, gathered itself together, effortlessly thrusting well in excess of the hundred-mph mark, eating up road without fuss or noise.

He had left London early on the Monday morning, and Ms. Proud was to be in the Casino each evening—from the Tuesday—between ten and eleven.

At a little after 6:00 P.M. on Tuesday the Mulsanne slid into Monaco's Place Casino and up to the entrance of the Hotel de Paris. It was a splendid, clear spring evening, with hardly a breath of wind to stir the palm trees in the gardens that front the Grand Casino. As he switched off the ignition, Bond checked that the small hidden weapon compartment below the polished wooden facia, to the right of the wheel, was locked; and that the safety key was turned on the powerful Super 1000 telephone housed between the front seats. Stepping out he glanced around the Place, nostrils filling with a mixture of bougainvillea, heavy French tobacco, and the soft sea air.

Monte Carlo—like the neighboring cities and towns along the Côte d'Azur—had a smell that was its own, and Bond reckoned someone could make a fortune if they could only bottle it, to provide nostalgic memories for those who had known the Principality in its heyday. For the one-time gambling legend of Europe was no longer the great romantic fairytale place remembered by people who had won, and lost, fortunes, and hearts, there in the old days. The packaged holiday, weekend tours and charter flights had put an end to that. Monaco only managed to keep up its veneer of sophistication through its royal family and the high prices that speculators, hoteliers, restaurateurs and shopkeepers could charge, and even these had not created an adequate buffer against some of the more garish attributes of the 1980s.

On his last visit, Bond had been stunned to find one-armed bandits installed even in the exclusive Salles Privées of the Casino. Now, he would not be surprised if there were Space Invader games there as well.

His room faced the sea and, before taking a shower and preparing for the evening, he stood on the balcony, looking out at the twinkling lights, sipping a martini and straining his ears, as though he might be capable of reaching out to recapture the sounds and laughter of former, brighter days.

After a modest dinner—a chilled consommé, grilled sole, and a mousse au chocolat—he went down to check the car, then walked over to the Casino, paying the entrance fee—which would admit him to the fabled Salles Privées—and purchasing fifty thousand francs worth of plaques, around four thousand pounds sterling.

There was play at only one of the tables, and, as he crossed the floor, he saw Ms. Proud for the first time. M had underestimated the case when he said her husband would not even recognize her. Bond, who had hardly credited the second picture—"the 'after' photograph," as M said—found it difficult to believe that the woman, undeniably the one from *that* photograph, could ever have been either plump or mousy.

She stood, bare-shouldered, her back against the bar, a tall, almost willowy figure, head tilted, small breasts thrusting into relief against the filmy material of her blue dress. Long ash-blonde hair just touched the tanned skin at the nape of her neck, and her light gray eyes were intent on the play at the table. The eyes were twinkling with amusement. A half smile hovered around her "new" mouth, full lips having replaced the original, while the once angular nose was now almost a snub.

Fascinating, Bond thought. Fascinating to see what strict diet, a nose job, contact lenses, and a dedicated course of beauty treatment and hairdressing could accomplish.

He did not pause on his way to the table, where he took a seat, acknowledging the croupier, and studied the game for three turns before dropping twenty-five thousand francs on *Impair.*

The croupier called the ritual *"Faites vos jeux,"* and all eyes watched, as the little ball bounced into the spinning wheel. *"Rien ne va plus."*

Bond glanced at the other three players—a smooth, American-looking man, late forties, blue-jowled and with the steely look of a professional gambler; a woman, in her early seventies, he judged, dressed in last season's fashions; and a heavyset Chinese whose face would never give away his age. Everyone followed the wheel now, as the ball bounced twice and settled into a slot.

"Dix-sept, rouge, impair et manque." the croupier intoned in that particular plainchant of the tables. Seventeen, red, odd and low.

The rake swung efficiently over the green baize, taking in the house winnings and pushing out plaques to the winners, including James Bond, whose *Impair* bet had netted him even money. At the call, he again placed twenty-five thousand on *Impair*. Once more he won: Eleven came up. *Impair* for a third time, and the ball rolled into fifteen. In three turns of the wheel, Bond had made seventy-five thousand francs. The other players were betting complex patterns—*A Cheval*, *Carré* and *Colonne*, which made for higher odds. James Bond was playing the easy way, high stakes for even returns. He pushed the whole of his seventy-five thousand onto *Pair* and fourteen—red— came up. Stake plus one hundred fifty thousand francs. Time to call it a night. He flipped a five thousand-franc plaque across the table, muttering *"Pour les employés,"* and pushed back the chair. There was a little squeal as the chair touched the girl's legs, and Bond felt liquid run down his left cheek where her drink had spilled—a natural enough incident, for the Englishman had not sensed her standing behind him. It was a move carefully prearranged far away in London, in the safe flat near St. Martin's Lane.

"I'm terribly sorry . . . *Pardon, Madam, je . . .*"

"It's okay, I speak English." The voice was pitched low, the accent clear and without any nasality. "It was my fault, I shouldn't have been standing so close. The game was very . . ."

"Well, at least let me get you a fresh drink." He completed drying off his face, took her elbow and steered her toward the small bar. One of the dinner-

37

jacketed security men smiled as he watched them go. Hadn't he seen women pick up men like this many times? No harm in it, as long as the women were straight, and this one was an American visitor. Silently he wished them luck.

"Mr. Bond," she said, raising her champagne cocktail to his.

"James. My friends call me James."

"And mine call me Percy. Persephone's too much of a mouthful."

Bond's eyes smiled over the rim of his glass. "Percy Proud?" An eyebrow cocked. "I'll drink to that."

Percy was a relaxed young woman, an easy communicator, and blessed with a sense of both humor and the ridiculous.

"Okay, James"—they were at last seated in her room at the Hotel de Paris, both armed with champagne cocktails—"down to cases. How much have you been told?"

"Very little." *She'll give you the fine print,* M had said. *Trust her; let her teach you. She knows more about all this than anyone.*

"You've seen this picture?" She extracted a small photograph from her handbag. "I just have to show it to you and then destroy. I don't want to be caught with it on me, thank you very much."

The photograph was a smaller print of the one they had shown him in the St. Martin's Lane safe flat.

"Jay Autem Holy," Bond said.

The man looked to be very tall, thinning hair failing to disguise a domed head, while the nose was large and beaky.

"*Doctor* Jay Autem Holy," she corrected.

"Deceased; and you are the widow—though I would scarcely have recognized you from the photos."

She gave a quick, melodic giggle. "There've been some changes made."

"I'll say. The other identity wouldn't have been attractive in black. The new one would look good in any color."

"Flattery could get you everywhere, James Bond. But I don't really think Mrs. Jay Autem Holy ever needed the widow's weeds. You see, he never died."

"Tell me."

She began with the story already told by M. Over a decade before, while Dr. Jay Autem Holy had been working solely for the Pentagon, a U.S. Marine Corps Grumman Mohawk aircraft had crashed into the Grand Canyon. It carried but two passengers: Holy and a General Joseph (Rolling Joe) Zwingli.

"You already know that Jay Autem was way ahead of his time," she said. "A computer whizz kid long before anyone had heard of computer whizz kids. He worked on very advanced programing for the Pentagon. The airplane went down in an almost inaccessible place—wreckage dumped deep into a crevasse. No bodies were ever recovered, and Jay Autem had a nice bundle of significant computer tapes with him when he went. Naturally, they were not recovered either. He was then working on a portable battle-training program for senior officers and had almost perfected a computerized system for anticipating enemy movements in the field. At that time his work was, literally, invaluable."

"And the general?"

"'Rolling Joe'? A nut. A much-decorated, and brave, nut. Believed the United States had gone to the dogs—the Commie Dogs. Said openly that there should be a change in the political system; that the Army should take control; the politicians had sold out; morals had gone to pieces; people had to be *made* to care."

Bond nodded, "And I gather Dr. Holy had a nickname—as 'Rolling Joe' was General Zwingli's nickname."

She laughed again. "They called Zwingli 'Rolling Joe' because, in World War II he had this habit of air-testing his B-17 Flying Fortress by rolling it at a thousand feet."

"And Dr. Holy?" he prompted.

"His colleagues, and some of his friends, called him 'The Holy Terror.' He could be a tough boss." Percy paused before adding, "And a tough husband."

"Late husband." Bond gave her a close, unblinking look and watched her drain the last of her champagne cocktail and place the glass carefully on a side table as she slowly shook her head.

"Oh, no," she said softly. "Jay Autem Holy did not die in that plane wreck. Certain people have been sure of that for some years. Now there's proof."

"Proof? Where?" He led her toward the moment for which M had prepared him.

"Right on your own doorstep, James. Deep in the English rural heart. Oxfordshire. And there's more to it than that. You remember the Kruxator robbery in London? And the £20 million gold bullion job?"

Bond nodded.

"Also the £2 billion air hijack? The British Airways 747 taking foreign currencies from the official printers in England to their respective countries?"

"Of course."

"You remember what those crimes had in common, James?"

He waved his gunmetal cigarette case at Percy, who declined with an almost imperceptible gesture of the hand. Bond was surprised to find the case being returned to his pocket unopened. His forehead creased.

"All large sums," he said. "Well planned . . . wait a minute, didn't Scotland Yard say they were almost computerized crimes?"

"That's it. You have the answer."

"Percy?" There was an edge of puzzlement in Bond's voice. "What are you suggesting?"

"That Dr. Jay Autem Holy is alive, and well, living in a small village called Nun's Cross, just north of Banbury, in your lovely Oxfordshire. Remember Banbury, James? The place where you can ride a cock horse to?" She made a tight movement of her lips. "Well, that's where he is. Planning criminal operations—and probably terrorist ones as well—by computer simulations."

"Evidence?"

"Well." Again a pause. "To say that no bodies were recovered in the plane wreck is not quite true. They got out the pilot's remains. There were no other bodies. Intelligence, security and police agencies have been searching for Jay Autem Holy ever since."

"And suddenly they found him in Oxfordshire?"

"Almost by chance, yes. One of your Special Branch men was in that area, on a completely different case. First he spotted a pair of well-known London crooks."

"And they led him to . . . ?"

Percy got up and slowly began to pace the room.

"They led him to a small computer games company called Gunfire Simulations, in the village of Nun's Cross, and there he sees a face from the files. So he goes back and checks. The face is that of Dr. Jay Autem Holy. Only now he calls himself Professor Jason St. John-Finnes—pronounced Sinjon-Finesse:

finesse, as in the game of bridge. The name of the house is Endor."

"As in Witch of?"

"Right."

Percy paused in her pacing and leaned over the back of Bond's armchair, her dress brushing his ear. He could not at that moment bring himself to turn his head and look up into the face above his shoulder.

"They even have chummy little weekend war-games house parties there, at which a lot of strange people turn up," Percy continued.

She rose and sidled over to a couch on to which she dropped, drawing her long slender legs up under her.

"Trouble was that none of this happened to be news to the American Service. You see, they've been keeping an eye on that situation for some time. Even infiltrated it, without telling anyone."

Bond smiled. "That would please my people no end. There are rules about operating on other countries' soil and—"

"As I understand it," Percy interrupted in a drawling voice, "there were what is known as frank and open discussions."

"I'll bet!" Bond thought for a moment. "Are you telling me that Jay Autem Holy—strongly prized by the Pentagon, and missing, believed dead—just managed to settle in this village, Nun's Cross, without benefit of disguise, or cover? Except for some new identity papers?"

Percy stretched out her legs and laid back almost full length on the couch, trailing her arm languidly and brushing the floor with her hand.

"Not an easy man to disguise," she said. "But, yes, that's exactly what he's done. Mind you he rarely goes out, he's hardly ever seen in the village. His so-called wife deals personally with business, and those he genuinely employs just think he's eccentric—which he is. A great deal of ingenuity and a lot of money went into fixing up Jay Autem's hideaway."

Slowly, many of the things M had said, back in London, started to make sense.

"And I'm the one who's supposed to join that happy band of brothers?" Bond asked.

"You've got it, in one."

"And just how am I supposed to do that? Walk in and say, Hi there, my name's James Bond, the famous renegade intelligence officer? I'm looking for a job."

It was Bond's turn to get up and pace the room.

"Something like that," Percy drawled softly.

"Good God!" Bond's face tightened in anger. "Of all the harebrained . . . Why would he want to employ me, anyway?"

"He wouldn't." She gave a flick of a smile and sat up, suddenly very alert and in earnest. "He's got enough staff to run the Gunfire Simulations business—all legal and aboveboard. And *are* they screened? It makes the British positive vetting look

like a kids' crossword puzzle. Believe me, I know. He
has to be certain, because that side of things is absolutely straight." She took a little breath, turning her
head slightly, like a singer swinging away from the
microphone. "No, James, he wouldn't think of em-
ploying you but there are people he works with who
just *might* find you a great temptation. That's what
your people are banking on."

"Mad. Absolute madness! How . . . ?"

"James," she soothed, standing up and taking both
his hands in hers. "You have friends at the court of
King St. John-Finnes—well, an acquaintance anyhow.
Freddie Fortune. The naughty Lady Freddie."

"Oh, Lord!" Bond dropped Percy's hands and
swung aside. Once, some years ago, Bond had made
the error of cultivating the young woman Percy had
just mentioned. In a way he had even courted her,
until he discovered that Lady Freddie Fortune—darling of the gossip columnists—suffered from a somewhat slapdash political education, which had placed
her slightly to the left of Fidel Castro.

"You also have to study, James. That's why you're
here, with me. To get an entree into Endor you must
know something about the job they do at Gunfire
Simulations. How much do you really know about
computers?"

Bond gave a sheepish smile. "If you put it like
that, the technicalities only."

Had he been pressed, computers were the last
thing he really wanted to discuss just then with the
strangely alluring and unsettling Persephone Proud.

– 5 –

Teacher's Pet

WITH A LUCIDITY born of his years in the Service, Bond outlined to Percy the way in which a microcomputer works, as they both sauntered about the room in almost a ritual dance, carefully avoiding one another. A complex electronic tool, designed to do particular tasks when a series of commands are read into its two memories, he annunciated in a toneless voice like a schoolboy reciting Latin declensions to an indulgent master. A machine that would keep records and work out financial tasks one minute, process data the next, receive and transmit information over thousands of miles in a matter of seconds; that would design your new house, or allow you to play complicated games, make music or display moving graphics. A miracle with an ever-growing memory, but only as good as the program it was given.

"I know the theory—just," Bond said with a smile. "But I haven't a clue how it's all done by the programer."

"That, as I understand it from your wonderful old boss, is the main reason we're here," Percy retorted. Bond was mildly surprised to hear M spoken of as his wonderful old boss. "My job is to teach you programing languages, with special reference to the kind of thing my dark angel of an ex-husband used to do, and probably is doing right now. Oh, yes, he is ex. Dead, missing, whatever, I made sure it was legal."

"And how difficult is that going to be?" Bond asked with feigned innocence.

"Depends on your aptitude. It's like swimming, or riding a bicycle. Once you've got the knack it becomes second nature. Mind you, we're up against a particular kind of genius when it comes to Jay Autem Holy. I'm going to have to tell you a lot about *him*. Seriously, though, it's simply like learning a new language, or how to read music."

Percy walked over to the closet, from which she hauled a pair of large, customized cases, heavily embellished with coded security locks. They contained a very large microcomputer, clearly of exceptionally advanced design, several types of disk drive, and three metal boxes, which, when opened, revealed disks of differing sizes. She asked Bond to move the

television set and then began to plug in the micro.
The keyboard was twice the size of that on an electronic typewriter. She talked as she set up the equipment. This micro, she told him, was her idea of what
Jay Autem would be using now. Bond had already
noticed that she referred to Dr. Holy simply as Jay
Autem or The Holy Terror.

"When he went missing, his own micro disappeared with him—or, I should say, at the same time. I
guess he had it stashed away somewhere safe. In
those days we were just beginning to see the full development of the microcompressor—you know, the
chip that put a whole roomful of computer circuits on
to a 5mm-square piece of silicon. He built his own
machine, and we were still mainly using tapes for
that. Since then there've been so many developments,
and things have become much smaller. I've tried to
keep pace with the technology, changing his original
design, doing my best to keep one jump ahead, as
he would have done. I rebuilt his Terror Six—
that's what he called his machine—and altered it as I
went on."

Bond stood peering over her shoulder as she
made final adjustments.

"This," she waved a hand at the console, "is my
equivalent of what would now be the Terror Twelve.
Since Jay Autem disappeared, the chips have gotten
smaller, but the big leap forward has been the incredible advance in the amount of memory a little

thing like this can contain. That, and the way more realistic pictures—real video—can be used in the kind of programs he's interested in."

"And what kind of programs are those, Percy?"

"Well—" she selected a disk from one of the boxes, switched on a drive, inserted the disk and powered up the machine "—I can show you the kind of thing that *used* to fascinate him, when he was doing work for the Pentagon. Then we can take it a stage further."

The television screen had come alive, the disk drive whirring and rasping, a series of rapid beeps emanating from the loudspeaker. The drive continued to grunt and honk when the staccato beeps finally stopped and the screen cleared, showing a detailed map of the border between East and West Germany—the district around Kassel, NATO country.

Unaccountably Bond suddenly felt hot and flushed. He almost reached out a hand to Percy's shoulder, but instead loosened his tie as she withdrew a heavy, functional black joystick from one of her cases and plugged it into the console, pressing the keyboard S. Immediately a bright rectangle appeared on the map, which, Bond saw, was as clear as a printed piece of cartography.

"Okay, this may look like some weird game to you, but I promise you, it's a very advanced training aid."

Percy activated the joystick, and the rectangle slid across the screen, moving the map as it reached the outer perimeter, so that it scrolled up and down. The entire area covered was about eighty square miles of border, with a long oblong blue window below the map.

"I type in coordinates, and we go immediately to that section of the map." Percy suited action to words, and the map jumped on the screen, the rectangle staying in place. "Now we can look at what is going on in a smaller area." She positioned the rectangle over a village, about a mile from the border, and pressed the trigger on the joystick. Bond had become aware of the perfume Percy was wearing but couldn't decide what it was. He jerked his mind back to the matter in hand.

It was as if a zoom lens had been applied to the screen, for now he could see detail—roads, trees, houses, rocks and fields. Among this detail Bond could pick out at least six tanks and four troop carriers, while a pair of helicopters sat hidden behind buildings, and three Harrier aircraft could be defined on pads shielded by trees.

"We have to assume that some form of non-nuclear hostility exists."

Percy was typing commands into the micro, asking for information, first on NATO forces. The tanks, troop carriers, helicopters and Harriers blinked in turn, while their designated call-signs and strength ribboned out on the lower part of the screen. Percy noted the call-signs on a pad at her elbow and then

typed a command for information concerning War-
saw Pact forces in this small sector, only a few miles
square.

They appeared to be facing at least two companies
of infantry, with armored support.

"It'll only give you available information, the kind
of thing intelligence and reconnaissance would actually have." Percy watched as the screen flashed up
known positions, the window running out data concerning the enemy.

Bond could not take his eyes from the soft curl of
her hair on an almost exposed shoulder as she began
to input orders. Two of the Harriers moved off, as
though flying in to attack the enemy armor. At the
same time, she activated the NATO tanks and troop
carriers.

Individual responses—from the tank and infantry
commanders—came up on the screen, while the tiny
vehicles moved to her bidding, the tanks suddenly
coming under attack, indicated by shell bursts on the
screen and audible crumps and whines. Bond
stooped slightly for a closer look at the screen and
found himself glancing sideways at Percy's face, pro-
filed and absorbed alongside his. He looked quickly
back at the screen.

The action, controlled throughout by Percy, lasted
for almost twenty minutes, during which time she was
able to gain a small superiority over the enemy forces

with the loss of three tanks, one helicopter, a Harrier and just under one hundred men.

Bond stood back a pace behind Percy. He had found the whole operation fascinating. He asked if this kind of thing was used by the military.

"This is only a simple computer TEWT," Percy said. A TEWT, she explained, was a Tactical Exercise Without Troops, a technique used in training officers and NCOs. "In the old days, as you know, they did TEWTs with boards, tables, sand trays and models. Now all you need is a micro. This is very simple, but you should see the advanced simulations they use at staff colleges."

"And Dr. Holy was programing this kind of thing for the Pentagon?" For the first time Bond noticed a little mole on Percy's neck that almost made him jump with delight.

"This, and more. When he disappeared, Jay Autem was into some exceptionally advanced stuff. Not only training but also specialist programs, where the computer is given all possible options and works out the one most likely to be taken by an opposing power under a particular set of circumstances."

"And now? If he really is still alive . . . ?"

"Oh, he's alive, James." She flushed suddenly. "I've seen him. Don't doubt it. He's the one I've already told you about—Jason St. John-Finnes, of

Nun's Cross, Oxfordshire. I should know. After all, I was his watchdog for three and a half lousy years . . ."

"Watchdog?" Her eyes really were the most incredible color, a subtle shade of turquoise that changed according to the light.

Percy looked away, biting her lip in mock shame. "Oh, didn't they tell you? I married the bastard under orders. I'm a Company lady—from Langley. Marriage to Dr. Holy was an assignment. How else would I know the inside of this operation?"

"He wasn't trusted, then?" Bond tried not to show surprise, even though the idea of a CIA employee being instructed to marry in order to keep surveillance on her husband appalled him.

"At that time, with his contacts—he had many friends among the scientific community in Russia and the Eastern bloc—they couldn't afford to trust him. And they were right."

"You think he's working for the KGB now?"

"No." She went to the small freezer to get another bottle of champagne. "No, Jay Autem worked for Jay Autem and nobody else. At least I discovered that about him." Passing another glass to Bond, she added, "There are almost certainly Soviet connections in what he's doing now, but it'll be on a freelance basis. Jay Autem knows his business, but he's really only dedicated to money. Politics is another matter."

"So what sort of thing do you reckon he's doing?" Bond caught another strong whiff of that strange perfume.

"As they say, James, that's for him to know, and you to find out. And it's my job to teach you how. Tomorrow morning we start, in earnest. Eight-thirty suit you?"

"Hardly worth my going back to my own room." Bond casually glanced at his watch.

"I know, but you're going all the same. I'm to teach you all I can about how to prepare the kind of programs Jay Autem writes, *and* give you a course on how to break into his programs, should you be lucky enough to get your hands on one."

Percy took hold of his wrist and reached up to kiss him gently on the cheek. Bond moved closer, but Percy stepped away, wagging a finger.

"That's a no-no, James. But I'm a good teacher, and, if you prove to be a diligent pupil, I have ways of rewarding you that you never dreamed of when you were at school. Eight-thirty, sharp. Okay?"

"You guarantee results, Proud Percy?"

"I guarantee to teach you, Bond James," she said with a wicked grin. "And about computer programing as well."

Promptly at eight-thirty the next morning, Bond knocked at her door, one arm hidden behind his back. When she opened up, he thrust out his hand to give her a large rosy apple.

"For the teacher," he smiled.

It was the only joke of the day, for Percy Proud proved to be a hard and dedicated taskmaster.

– 6 –

Holy Code

IT TOOK A LITTLE LESS than a month, and even that was a tribute to Persephone Proud's teaching skill, as well as her pupil's capabilities. For the job—as they both knew—entailed the equivalent of learning a new language, and several complicated dialects in addition. Indeed, James Bond could not remember a time when he had been forced to call so heavily on his mental reserves, to focus his concentration, like a burning glass, on the intellectual matter at hand.

They quickly established a routine, which seldom varied. For the first few days they worked from eight-thirty each morning, but, as the late nights began to take their toll, this was modified to ten o'clock.

They would work until around one, then take lunch in a nearby bar, walking there and back, then resume work until five.

Each evening, at seven, they would go down to Le Bar—the Hotel de Paris' famous meeting place, where, it is said, the wrists and necks of the ladies put the Cartier showcases to shame.

If they intended to stay in Monaco for the evening, the couple would dine in the hotel, but further afield they could be seen at L'Oasis in La Napoule when the Cannes Casino took their fancy, sampling the latest tempting dish invented by the gourmet master chef, Louis Outhier. Sometimes they took a more austere meal at the Negresco in Nice, or even at La Réserve in Beaulieu, or—on occasions—the modest Le Galion, at the Menton port of Garavan. Wherever they ate, the meal was always a prelude to a night at the tables. *Don't go invisible*, M had instructed. *You are bait, and it would be a mistake to forget it. If they're trawling there, let them catch you.* So, the Bentley Mulsanne Turbo slid its silent way along the coast roads each evening, and the tanned, assured Englishman and his willowy elegant American companion became familiar figures on the gambling landscape of the Côte d'Azur.

Bond played only the wheel, and then conservatively—though he tended to double up on bets, plunging heavily on some evenings, coming away thousands to the good on others. Mainly he worked to a system using big money on the *Pair, Impair, Manque* and *Passe,* which paid evens, only occasionally changing to a *Carré*—covering four numbers at odds of just over eight to one.

Within the first week, he was the equivalent of a few thousand pounds, sterling, to the good, and knew the various casinos were watching with interest. No casino—even with the reputation of those along that once glittering coast—is happy about a regular who plays systematically, and wins.

Most nights, Percy and Bond were back at the hotel between three and three-thirty in the morning. Occasionally it was earlier—even one o'clock—giving them a chance to do another hour's work before getting a good sleep before starting all over again.

From time to time, during those weeks, they would not return until dawn—driving the coast roads with windows open to scent the morning air, feasting their eyes on the greenery of palm and plane trees, cacti and the climbing flowers around the summer homes of the wealthy, with their swimming pools fed by spouting marble dolphins. On those occasions, they would get back to the hotel in time to smell the first coffee of the day—one of the most satisfying aromas in the world, Bond thought.

The hotel staff considered it all very romantic—the attractive American lady and the wealthy Englishman (so lucky at the tables, and in love). Nobody would have dreamed of disturbing the lovebirds.

The truth concerning their enclosed life in Percy's room was, in fact, far removed from the fantasies of chambermaids and porters—at least for the first couple of weeks.

Percy began by teaching Bond how to flowchart a program—to draw out, in a kind of graph, exactly what he wanted the program to do. This he mastered in a matter of forty-eight hours, after which the serious business of learning the Basic computer language began. There were extra lessons on the use of graphics and sound. Toward the end of the second week, Bond started to learn various dialects of Basic, gradually grasping the essentials of further, more complex, languages like Machine Code, Cobal, or the high-level Pascal, and Forth.

Even in their spare time, they spoke of little else but the job in hand, though usually with special reference to Jay Autem Holy, and it did not take long for Bond to glean that Holy used his own hybrid program language, which Percy referred to as Holy Code.

"It's one of Jay Autem's main strengths as far as protecting his programs is concerned," Percy told him over dinner. "He's still using the same system, and the games being produced by his little company—Gunfire Simulations—are quite inaccessible to other programers. He always said that, if security was necessary—and by God he believed in it—the simplest protection is the best. He has an almost perfect little routine at the start of all his games programs, one that's quite unreadable by anyone who wants to copy, or get into the disk. It's probably the same piece of code he used to put on to his Pentagon work. Anyone trying to copy, or list, turns the disk into gibberish."

Bond insisted on talking about Dr. Holy whenever he was given the opportunity, for Percy was as close as he could ever get to knowing the man, before meeting him.

"He looks like a great angry hawk: Well, you've seen the photographs." They were dining in the hotel. "Outward appearances are not to be trusted, though. If I hadn't been on a specific job, I could easily have fallen for him. In fact, in some ways I did. There were often times when I hoped he'd prove to be straight." She looked pensive, and, for a moment, it was as though she saw neither Bond nor their plush surroundings. "He has amazing powers of concentration. That knack of being able to close the world out and allow his own work to become the only reality. You know how dangerous that can be."

Bond reflected that it could produce the kind of madness that turned men into devils, and Percy agreed. "Oh, yes, kind, loving and generous one minute: a clawing, ranting, terrifying ogre the next."

It was after this particular dinner, toward the end of the second week, that two things happened, one of which was to change the even tenor of Bond's emotions for some time to come.

"So, are we playing the Salles Privées tonight, or shall we jaunt?" Percy asked.

Bond decided on a trip along the coast, to the small casino in Menton, and they left soon after.

The gaming itself did not make it a night to remember, though Bond came away with a few thousand extra francs in his wallet.

As they pulled away from the casino, taking the road through Carnoles and so back to Monaco, he caught the lights of a car drawing away from directly behind him. He hadn't noticed anybody getting into it. Immediately he told Percy to tighten her seatbelt.

"Trouble?" She betrayed no sign of nervousness.

"I'm going to find out." He gunned the big car forward, letting it glide steadily into the nineties, holding well into the side of the narrow road.

The lights of the car behind remained visible, and when he was forced to slow—for that particular road twists and turns before hitting the long stretch of two-lane highway—it came closer, a white Citroen, its distinctive snout clearly visible behind its lowered headlight. It stuck like a limpet, a discreet distance behind. Bond wondered if it might only be some Frenchman, or an Italian wanting to race or showing off to a girlfriend. Yet the prickling sensation around the back of his neck told him this was a more sinister challenge.

They came off the two-lane stretch of highway like a rocket, and Bond stabbed at the big footbrake in order to drop speed quickly. The road into Monaco was not only narrow but also closed in on both sides, by rockface or houses, leaving little room for maneuver.

The Bentley's speed dropped and he took the next bend at around sixty. Percy gave a little audible intake of breath and, as he heard her, so Bond saw the obstruction: another car, pulled over to the right but still in the Bentley's road space, its hazard lights winking like a dragon's eyes. To its left, hardly moving and blocking most of the remaining space, was an old and decrepit lorry, wheezing and chugging as though about to suffer a complete collapse. He yelled for Percy to hang on, jabbed hard at the brake and slewed the Bentley, first left, then right, in an attempt to slalom his way between the vehicles. Halfway through the right-hand skid, it was plain they would not make it. The Bentley's engine howled as he pushed the stalk from automatic drive to low-range, taking the engine down to first.

They were both jarred against the restraining straps of their seatbelts as the heavy machinery halted in midlunge, the speed dropping from fifty-five almost to zero in the blink of an eye. They were angled across the road with the car jamming their right side and the elderly lorry now backing slightly on the left. Pincers. Before they could take any further action, two men jumped down from the lorry and another pair materialized from the shadows surrounding the parked car, while the white Citroen boxed them in neatly from behind.

"Doors!" Bond shouted, slamming his hand against his door lock control, knowing his warning was more of a precaution than anything else, for the central locking system should be in operation. At least three of the team now approaching the Bentley appeared to be armed with axes.

Reaching for the hidden pistol compartment catch, Bond realized even as he did it, was only a reflex action. If he operated the electric window to use the weapon, they had a route in. They could get in anyway, for even a car built like this would eventually collapse under well-wielded axes.

The Bentley Mulsanne Turbo is a little over six-and-a-half feet wide. This one was not quite at right angles across the road. The Citroen behind, Bond judged, was within a foot of his rear bumper, but the Bentley's weight would compensate for that. Ahead, the car with its hazard lights blinking was a couple of inches from his door, the lorry some three inches from the bonnet. Directly in front, eight feet or so away, the roadside reached up into a sloping rock face. The Bentley's engine had not stalled, and still gave out its low grumble.

Holding his foot hard on the brake pedal, Bond adjusted the wheel, and, as one of the assailants came abreast of his window, placing himself between the Mulsanne and the parked car, raising both hands to bring down the axe, Bond slid the gear stalk into reverse, lifting his foot smartly off the brake.

The Bentley slid backwards, fast. Then a judder as they hit the Citroen, and a yelp of pain, loud and clear, from the man about to try to force entry with his axe. Thrown to one side, he had been crushed between the Bentley and the parked car.

With a quick movement, Bond now slid the automatic gear into drive. He had at most an extra six inches to play with and his foot bore gently down on the accelerator.

The car eased forward. Once again the screaming attacker on their right was crushed as the Bentley straightened, then gathered speed and headed for the gap.

The steering on the Mulsanne Turbo is so light and accurate that Bond did not have to wrench at the wheel; he simply used a very light touch of his fingers. The car gathered speed as it closed into the narrow gap between lorry and car. More control to the left. Straight. Hard left. A fraction to the right. Now! His foot went down, and they hurtled forward, clearing the front of the car with less than an inch to spare between the lorry on the left and the rock face to the right.

Then, quite suddenly, they were through, and

back on the main, empty road, shooting downhill into Monaco itself.

"Hoods?" He could feel Percy quivering beside him.

"You mean *our* kind?" Bond replied. "Lion tamers?"

She nodded, her mouth forming a small "Yes."

"Don't think so. Looked like a team out to take our money and anything else they could grab. There's always been plenty of that along this coast. In the north of England they have a saying—where there's muck there's money. You can change that to where there's money there's lice."

Deep down, though, Bond knew he was lying. It was just possible that the cars, lorry and team were a group of gangsters, but the setup had been deadly in its professionalism and sophistication. He would report it as soon as he could get a safe line to London. Aloud he told Percy that he would do just that.

"So shall I."

They said nothing more until they got to her room. After that, neither of them would ever be able to say what started it.

"They were pros," she said.

"Yes."

"Don't like it, James. I'm pretty experienced, but I can still get frightened."

She moved toward him, and in a second his arms were around her, and their lips met as though each was trying to breathe fresh energy into the other. Her mouth slid away from his, and her cheek lay alongside his neck as she clung, whispering his name.

So they became lovers, their needs and feelings adding urgency to every moment of their days and nights. And so came a fresh anxiety. The final goal loomed before them: preparing Bond to meet Percy's former husband.

At the start of the third week, Percy suddenly called a halt. "I'm going to show you the kind of thing that Jay Autem could well be writing now," she announced, switching off the Terror Twelve and removing the set of normal disk drives that Bond had just been using.

In their place she fitted a large, hard-disk laser drive, and powering up the system, booted a program into the computer.

What appeared on the screen now were not the standard computer graphics Bond had become used to, even in their highest form, but genuine pictures— real, natural in color and texture, like a controllable movie.

"Video," Percy explained. "A camera interfaced with a hard laser computer disk. Now watch!"

She manipulated the joystick controller, and it was as though they were driving along a city street in heavy traffic.

Certainly the human forms she produced during the demonstration were more like advanced cartoon characters than the genuine background against which she made them move, run and fight. But the difference—using these symbolic figures against genuine places—added an almost frightening reality.

"I call it Bank Robbery," Percy said, and there was no doubt about the intention. By the clever juxtaposition of real film and graphics, you could "play" at robbing a real bank, dealing with every possible emergency that might arise. Bond was more than impressed.

"When I've taught you how to process and copy Jay Autem's work, you'll have the Terror Twelve and three types of drive to take with you, James. Don't say I haven't provided you with all the essential creature comforts. Now, let's really get to it."

Until later that evening, Bond applied himself to the work, but his mind hovered between the tasks at hand and the appalling tool that Jay Autem Holy—or indeed anyone with the necessary knowledge—had at his disposal for evil. Certainly Bond had been aware of the vast changes the micro had made in business, police and security work, but never before had he considered how far the applications of these machines had leaped forward. It should have been obvious, of course. If there were programs to assist the military in learning strategy and tactics, there had to be the possibility of those through which people could learn the best way to rob, cheat and even kill. The idea, combined with Percy's incredible demon-

stration of "living graphics"—in the shape of video
pictures being combined with a game-type program—had brought new dimensions to his own
thinking.

"And you really believe training programs, like
the one you showed me earlier, are being used by
criminals?" he asked much later, when they were in
bed.

"I'd be very surprised if they were not." Percy's
face was grave. "Just as I'd be amazed if Jay Autem
was not training criminals, or even terrorists, in his
nice Oxfordshire house." She gave a humorless little
laugh. "I doubt if it's called Endor by accident. The
Holy Terror has a dark sense of humor."

Bond knew that she was almost certainly right.
Every two days, he received a report from England,
via Bill Tanner: a digest of the information coming
from the surveillance team that had been set up, with
exceptionally discreet care, in the village of Nun's
Cross. The reports showed that not only criminals but
also known link-men with terrorist organizations
from the Middle East, Italy, Germany and even closer
to home were in constant contact with Professor St.
John-Finnes and his small team of assistants at Endor.
The sooner he got back to England and insinuated
himself into that hornet's nest, the better it would be.
London wanted him back, and even though they assured him the incident on the road between Menton

and Monaco could only be the work of local gangsters, Bond detected a fresh anxiety.

He even asked Percy what she thought had actually happened on the night Dr. Holy went missing, and she gave a snort. "Well, he certainly didn't go by himself. That should be obvious to a cretin. Dear old Rolling Joe Zwingli must have gone with him, and that guy was as mad as a hatter—they had a file long as your arm on him at Langley. Oh, he was brave, in that foolhardy, unimaginative way some soldiers are, but, as I told you at the start, he was also crazy. Became very bitter after Viet Nam. He turned exceptionally, violently anti-American, so he was just the kind of malleable character Jay Autem could have used to set up a disappearing act."

"Dealt with the pilot first, then jumped, I suppose?" Bond was almost speaking to himself.

Percy nodded, then shrugged. "And did away with Rolling Joe when it suited him."

Bond finished Percy's course two days early having mastered the art of copying all types of programs, even those protected by every method Percy knew to be used by Dr. Holy. They saved the last two days for themselves.

"You're an enchantress," Bond told her. "I know of nobody else who could have taught me so much in such a short time."

"You've given me a few wrinkles as well, and I don't mean on my face," Percy said, putting her head back onto the pillow. "Come on, James, darling, one more time—as the jazzmen say—then we'll have a sumptuous dinner, and you can really show me how to play those tables in the Salles Privées." It was mid-afternoon, and by nine that evening they were both seated at the first table in the Casino's most sacred of rooms.

Bond's run of luck was still high, though he was now gambling with care, harboring his winnings, which had quadrupled since his arrival. During the three hours they played that night he was, at one point, down to forty thousand francs. But the wheel started to run in his favor, and eventually, by midnight, his winnings had increased to three hundred thousand francs.

He waited for two turns to pass, deciding to make the next bet the last of the night, when he heard a sharp intake of breath from Percy.

Glancing toward her, he saw the color leave her face, the eyes shocked and staring at the entrance. It was not so much a look of fear as one of surprise.

"What is it?"

She answered in a whisper. "Let's get out. Quickly. Over there. Just come in."

"Who?" His eyes fell on a tall, grizzled man, straight-backed, and with eyes that swept the room as though surveying a battlefield. He did not really need to hear her reply.

"The old devil. And we thought Jay Autem had

done him in. That's Rolling Joe in the flesh. Joe Zwingli's here, and with a couple of infantry divisions by the look of it!"

Zwingli was now moving into the room, flanked by four other men, neat and smart as officers on parade, and looking as dangerous as an armored brigade about to attack a Boy Scout troop.

– 7 –

Rolling Home

GENERAL JOE ZWINGLI had been no chicken at the time of his disappearance. He must now be in his middle, or, more probably, late seventies. Yet, from where Bond sat, Rolling Joe looked like a man of sixty, in good physical shape. The other four men were younger, heavier, and not the kind of people you would be likely to meet at Sunday School parties.

For a moment, Bond sat calmly awaiting the worst, convinced that Zwingli and his men were looking for him and Percy. There had to be a connection; one didn't need a crystal ball to work that out. Zwingli had gone missing with Jay Autem Holy, so had been a necessary part of the disappearance plot. If there was collusion at the time of the airplane wreck, there would still be collusion now—for Dr. Holy and General Zwingli were tied together for life, by a much stronger bond than the marriage vows. Conspirators can rarely divorce.

Bond smiled genially. "Don't stare, Percy, it's rude. It also may call the good general's attention to us—if it's us he's looking for." His lips hardly moved as he watched Zwingli and his entourage out of the corner of one eye.

To his relief, the general's craggy face broke into a broad smile. He was not looking in their direction but advancing toward a dark-skinned, muscular man, possibly in his middle thirties, who had been sitting at the bar.

The pair shook hands, warmly, and there were greetings and introductions all round.

"I think, to be on the safe side, it would be prudent for us to take our leave now," Bond muttered. "Be casual and natural."

He went through the business of tipping the croupier, gathering the plaques together as they rose and made their way to the *caisse*, where Bond opted for cash rather than a check. Once outside, he took Percy's arm, leading her firmly back to the hotel.

"It could simply be coincidence, but I'm taking no chances. I don't for a moment think he could recognize you. How well did you know him, Percy?"

"Two or three dinner parties. Washington social functions. I knew him, but he always gave the impression of being completely uninterested. Not just in me, but in all women. It was him all right, James. I've no doubt about that."

During M's briefing Bond had studied a number of photographs, including the two well-documented occasions when General Zwingli had appeared on the cover of *Time* magazine. "For someone who's been dead that long, he looked in exceptionally good shape. No, the only way he could recognize you is if he was forewarned; if he knew you'd changed your . . . well . . . your image."

Percy giggled. "This *is* my real image, James. Mrs. Jay Autem Holy was the disguise. I ate my head off, let my hair go, wore plain, thick, clear-glass spectacles to make it look like I had the worst eyesight since Mr. Magoo . . ."

"And the nose?"

"Okay, so I had a nose job after Jay Autem went missing—nobody's perfect. But you're right, I'd have had to be fingered directly to Rolling Joe for him to know it was me."

"There's always the possibility that someone's fingered *me*." Bond brushed back the lock of hair that fell, like a comma, over his right eye. They reached the hotel entrance. "You recognize the fellow he met? The swarthy one the general seemed to be expecting?"

"The face was familiar. I've seen him—or a picture of him—before. Maybe he's on file. You?"

"The same. I should know him." Bond continued to talk, telling her they would have to leave, ". . . and fast. It's only a precaution, but we really shouldn't hang around. The best way would be for us both to get away in the Bentley. We can be in Paris by lunchtime tomorrow."

"Wait till we're upstairs," she said, then when they reached her room: "My brief was to leave here on my own. I have a car, and orders that we go separately. Under no circumstances are we to travel together. Those are my instructions, and there's no way I'm going to disobey them."

"So?"

"So I agree with you, James. I think it's merely a coincidence. It's also a useful piece of information— knowing that Zwingli lives. And I think we should leave: the sooner, the better."

They went their different ways, to pack. Bond lugged the cases containing the Terror Twelve into his own room, together with the various disk drives and several utility programs, on disks, to help him copy, or recover, Holy's listings—should he get hold of any. Meanwhile he worried at the identity of the man Zwingli had met in the Salles Privées. Automatically he had broken down the description of him so that his mind registered the main features: average height, muscular, dark-skinned, almost certainly of Middle Eastern origin. Regular, rather straight, nose; neat heavy black hair cut short; eyes to match, set wide on the squarish face; lips normal, no thickness; a small mustache; moved confidently; could have a military background. Worry at it, Bond told himself, and the name will come.

Percy settled her bill separately, and they met, as planned, in the garage, after her luggage had been loaded into the boot of her sporty little blue Dodge 600ES.

They would both be traveling on roughly the same road, for Percy had to return to the CIA Paris Station, while Bond faced the long drive back to Calais, and the ferry to Dover.

"You think we'll ever meet again?" Bond felt uncharacteristically inadequate.

She put her hands on his shoulders, looking into the startlingly blue eyes. "We have to, don't we, James?"

He nodded, knowing they shared each other's private thoughts. "You know how to get in touch with me?"

It was her turn to give a small nod. "Or you can call me—when all this is over." She rattled off a Washington number. "If I'm not there, they'll pass on a message, okay?"

"Okay." He stepped forward, and Percy put her arms around his neck, kissing him, long and lovingly on the mouth.

As she started up the Dodge, Percy leaned out of the window: "Take care, James. I'll miss you." Then she was gone, in a smooth acceleration, along the lane of cars and out—up the ramp—into the streets of Monaco, and the night roads of France.

Half an hour later, as planned, Bond took the Mulsanne Turbo from the same garage, and, within minutes, he was out of the Principality, heading back along the Moyenne Corniche toward the beginning of the main A8 Autoroute.

It was on the first leg—at about four in the morning—when Bond suddenly remembered the true identity of the man Zwingli had met. Yes, there *was* a file. The thick dossier had been across Bond's desk on several occasions, and there was a general watching brief on Tamil Rahani. Part American, part Lebanese, and carrying at least two passports, Rahani was usually in New York, where he was chairman, and principal shareholder, of Rahani Electronics. He had first come to the attention of the Service some five years before, handed on to them by their American counterparts. At this time, Rahani made several attempts to secure defense contracts from both the American and British governments, mainly in connection with aircraft communications electronics.

They had turned Rahani down flat, mainly because of his many contacts with undeniably unfriendly agencies, and uncertain governments. Wealthy; smooth; sharp; intelligent, and slippery as an eel. The flag on the file—Bond remembered—was ciphered *Possible clandestine. Probable subversive.*

78

Once the truth had settled in his mind, Bond pushed the Mulsanne to its limit. All he wanted to do was get back to England, report to M, and try to move in on Jay Autem Holy—a task that was more inviting than ever, now that he knew something of the doctor's work, plus the fact that Zwingli was alive, well, and—unless he was mistaken—working hand in glove with a highly suspect character.

During the final stage of the long drive—on the Autoroute to Calais—Bond found himself singing aloud. Perhaps, after the enforced idleness, lack of excitement, and intrigues of M's plan to use him as bait, he was starting to feel the fire of action in his belly once more.

"Rolling home," he sang, remembering far-off days when he would literally roll home, with brother officers.

"Rolling home,
By the light of the silvery moon;
I have twopence to lend,
And twopence to spend,
And twopence to send home to . . ."

His voice trailed off. He could not bring himself to sing the last line, about sending money home to his wife. For the ghost of his own dead wife, Tracy, still haunted him, even though he consciously missed Percy Proud's clear mind and agile, beautiful body.

Weakness, he chided himself. He was trained as a loner, one who acted without others, one who relied on himself. Yet he did miss her . . .

Pull yourself together, he told himself. Yet, undeniably, there were moments when he thought he could still smell her scent, and touch her skin.

Among the bills and circulars of mail awaiting Bond at his London flat was one letter—from a firm of business consultants—that demanded special attention. Embedded within this seemingly innocuous letter were a series of telephone numbers—one for each day of the week—that he could ring and so set up a meeting at the safe house near St. Martin's Lane.

This time it was a truly glorious late spring evening. Summer was around the corner, and you could feel it, even in the heart of the capital.

"Well, 007, the woman's taught you all the tricks of the trade, eh?"

"Some of them, sir. But I really wanted to talk to you about a new development." Without wasting words, or time, he gave them a summary of the final hours in Monaco, and the sighting of Zwingli with Tamil Rahani.

Bond had hardly got Rahani's name out before M ordered the Chief of Staff to check.

"There's a spot and report order on that joker." M looked at Bond, the old gray eyes hard and showing no compassion.

80

Tanner returned within ten minutes. "Last report from Milan. Seen by our resident there, who had a weather eye on him. Rahani appeared to be on his usual round of business meetings." The Chief of Staff gave a somewhat downcast shrug. "Unhappily, sir, nobody spotted him leaving. Though his airline ticket showed a return booking to New York yesterday, he was not on the flight."

"And I suppose nobody's seen hide nor hair of him since?" M nodded like a Buddha. "Except 007, in Monaco."

"Well, he was in the casino," Bond added. "As I've said, with General Zwingli and four thugs."

M looked at him, in silence, for a full minute. "Incredible," he said, "incredible that Zwingli's still alive, let alone mixed up with Rahani. Where does *he* fit into all this? You'll just have to be alert to Rahani's possible involvement, 007. He's always been a bit of an unknown quantity, so we'll inform those who need to know. You see, we're ready to put you in. Now, here's what I want you to do. First, your old acquaintance Freddie Fortune has . . ."

James Bond groaned loudly.

For the next week, he was to be seen around his old London haunts. He confided in one or two people that his feelings of disillusion had grown considerably. He had been in Monte Carlo where things had run true to the old adage—lucky at cards, unlucky in love—except it had been roulette, not cards.

Carefully, he laid a trail among people most likely to talk, or those whose connections were right for some "salting." Then, on the Thursday evening, in the bar of one of Mayfair's plush caravanserai, he bumped, as if by accident, into Lady Freddie Fortune, the extravagant, extreme, pamphlet-wagging socialite, whom he always called his "Champagne Communist." She was a vivacious, petite, compact and pretty redhead, completely untrustworthy, and always in the gossip columns, either campaigning for some outrageous cause or involved in sexual scandal. "Red Freddie," as some called her, was discreet only when it suited her. That night, Bond dropped a hint that he was now looking for work in the computer field. He also poured out all his troubles—an affair in Monte Carlo that had ended disastrously, leaving him bitter and wretched.

Lady Freddie was, it seemed, titillated to see this man, once a pillar of good form, become so emotional, so she whipped Bond off to her bed, allowing him to cry on her shoulder, which led, inevitably to other acts of sympathy. The next morning, Bond feigned a hangover and a morose, even waspish, manner. But none of this put Freddie Fortune off in the slightest. As he was leaving, she told him that she had some particular friends who might well be of use to him. If, that is, he really meant to find a job in computers.

"Here." She tucked a small business card into his

breast pocket. "It's a nice little hotel. If you can make it on Saturday, I'll be there. Only, for heaven's sake, don't let on I've told you. I leave it to you, James, but, if you do decide to come, be surprised to see me. Okay?"

On the following Saturday morning, therefore—with a weekend case and all the computer equipment in the boot of the Bentley—James Bond drove out of London, onto the Oxford road. Within the hour he had turned off and was threading through country lanes, heading for the village of Nun's Cross, near Banbury.

– 8 –

The Bull

BANBURY CROSS IS NOT AN ANTIQUITY, but was erected in the late 1850s, to commemorate the marriage of the Princess Royal to the Crown Prince of Prussia. There was a much earlier cross—there were three, to be exact—but the present Victorian Gothic monstrosity was placed where it is today because a local historian believed this to be the site of the ancient High Cross.

Three miles to the north of Banbury, nestling beside a wooded hill, lies the village of Nun's Cross, and there is no cross on view there at all.

James Bond guided the Mulsanne Turbo through the narrow main street of Nun's Cross, and into the yard of the coaching inn, which rejoices in the name of The Bull at the Cross.

The inn, he considered, hefting the overnight case from the boot, was probably the only going concern in Nun's Cross—a beautiful Georgian building, lovingly kept, and neatly modernized. The Bull, he'd noted in a guidebook, even offered "gourmet weekends for the discriminating."

From the porter who took his case, Bond learned that, as far as the hotel was concerned, it was going to be a very quiet weekend.

"A strange paucity of bookings, sir," the porter told him. "Possibly the recession. Jammed full last weekend, and booked to the rafters next. But now it's very sparse—thank you, sir," as the tip changed hands. "We've had a lot of the recession around here, sir."

Bond unpacked, changed into gray slacks, an open-necked shirt topped by a navy pullover, and his most comfortable moccasins. He was not armed. The ASP 9mm lay comfortably clipped into its hidden compartment in the Bentley. Yet he remained alert as he went down, through the old coach yard and into the village street. His eyes were searching for either a dark blue Jaguar XJ6 or a gray Mercedes-Benz saloon. The license numbers had been committed to memory, for both cars had appeared in his mirror, exchanging places with monotonous frequency, ever since he had taken to the road that morning.

He was under no illusion. For the first time since he had assumed the mantle of a disaffected former member of the Secret Service, someone other than his own people was following him—almost blatantly, for it was as though they wished to be seen as well as to see.

It was too early for a lunchtime drink. Bond decided to have a look around this village, which, if everything added up, harbored a sophisticated villain who was possibly also a traitor.

The Bull at the Cross lay almost on the crossroads that marked the center of the old village—a hodgepodge of mainly Georgian buildings, with a sprinkle of slightly older terraces, houses that were now the village shops, leaning in on one another as though mutually dependent. Small rows of what must, at one time, have been laborers' cottages now housed those who commuted into Banbury, or even Oxford, to labor in different fields.

Almost opposite the coach yard entrance stood the church, while, to the south, the main street meandered out into open country, scattered with copses and studded with larger houses. Gateways and rhododendron-flanked drives gave glimpses of large, sedate Victorian mansions, or glowing Hornton stone Georgian buildings. The third driveway past the church was walled, with heavy, high and modern gates set into the original eighteenth-century stone. A small brass plate was sunk into the wall to the right of the gates: Gunfire Simulations Ltd. In newer stone, carved and neatly blended with the original, was the one word "Endor."

The drive, which turned abruptly into a turmoil of low trees and bushes, appeared to be neatly kept, and a slash of gray slate roof was only just visible some two hundred yards in the distance.

Bond calculated that the grounds were about a square mile in extent, for the high wall continued to his left, the boundary being a narrow dirt track neatly signposted "The Shrubs."

After half a mile or so, he turned back, retracing his steps along the village street and carrying on to the northern extremity, where the cluster of old houses bordered on a scrubby, wooded hill. Here the sharp speculators had been at work and a modern housing estate—as many small brick boxes as possible in the space—had encroached almost on the woodland itself.

It was after twelve when Bond ambled slowly back to the inn. The dark blue Jaguar stood not far from the Bentley. Only the staff appeared to be about. He even found the private bar empty, but for the barman and one other guest.

"James, darling, what a surprise to find *you* here, out in the sticks!" Freddie Fortune, neat in an emerald shirt and tight jeans, sat in a window seat.

"The surprise is mutual, Freddie. Drinking?"

"Vodka and tonic, darling."

He got the drinks from the barman, carrying them over to Freddie, saying loudly, "What brings you here, then?"

"Oh, I adore this place. Come down to commune with nature—and friends—about once a month. Not your sort of place though, James." Then, quietly, "So glad you could make it."

Bond said he was glad also, although he felt unutterably foolish, chattering after the manner of Freddie's usual London friends.

Freddie took a quick sip of her vodka and tonic. "So you wanted to get out of the hurlyburly, yah?"

"Yah," Bond almost mimicked her affected accent.

"Or did you come because *I* asked you?"

He gave a noncommittal "Mmmm."

"Or, perhaps, the possibility of work?"

"Little of all three, Freddie."

"Three's a crowd." She snuggled up beside him. Freddie's small, excellently proportioned figure was just right for snuggling, thought Bond. Then—almost immediately—his face clouded—as Persephone entered his mind, so clearly that she might really have been there in person. For a second, Bond had a strange, eldritch feeling that Percy was genuinely close by.

They lunched together from a menu that would not have put the Connaught to shame, then walked for some five miles across the fields and through the woodland, getting back around three-thirty—"Just in time for a nice quiet siesta." Freddie gave him the come-to-bed look, and Bond, invigorated by the walk, did not stand a chance. When he entered her room, she was lying on the bed, wearing precious little.

Smiling sweetly, she said, "Come and bore the pants off me, darling."

"Dinner together?" Bond asked later, as they sat over tea in the Residents' Lounge. The hotel had filled up, and three Spanish waiters scurried about with silver teapots, small plates of sandwiches and fancy cakes.

"Oh, Lord, darling," Freddie put on her "devastated" face. "I have a dinner date." Then she smiled—sweet innocence. "So have you, if we play our cards right. You see—I told you so—I've got some old friends who live here." She suddenly became confidential. "Now, listen, James, they could be a godsend. You were serious about going into computers? Programing and all that sort of thing? Micros?"

"Absolutely."

"Super. Old Jason'll be thrilled."

"Jason?"

"My friend—well, friends really. Jason and Dazzle St. John-Finnes."

"Dazzle?"

Freddie gave an impatient back-flip of her hand. "Oh, I think her real name's Davide or something

90

peculiar. Everyone calls her Dazzle. Super people. Into computers in a really big way. They're incredibly clever and invent frightfully complicated war games."

M had already briefed him about the other members of Jay Autem Holy's entourage—the "wife," Dazzle; a young expert called Peter Amadeus ("Austrian, I think," Freddie now added); and the even younger Cambridge graduate, Ms. Cindy Chalmer.

"She's an absolute hoot." Freddie became expansive. "The local peasants call her Sinful Cindy, and she's jolly popular, particularly with the men. Black, you know."

No, Bond said he did not know, but he would like to find out. How did Sinful Cindy get on with Peter Amadeus?

"Oh, darling, no woman has anything to fear—or hope for—from the Amadeus boy, if you see what I mean. Look, I'll give Jason a bell." Freddie, like many of her kind, was apt to lapse into the London vernacular, particularly when out of Town. "Just to make certain they don't mind me having you in tow."

She disappeared for five minutes or so.

"We've got a result, James," she gushed on her return. "They'd absolutely adore to have you as a dinner guest."

Gently he questioned her, in an attempt to discover how long "Old Jason and Dazzle" had been such close friends. She hedged a little, but it finally transpired that she had known them for exactly two months.

They went in the Bentley—"I adore the smell of leather in a Rolls, or Bentley. So positively sexual," Freddie said, curled up in the front passenger seat. Playing out the charade, he was careful to ask for directions, and as they neared the turning she told him—"The gates'll probably be closed, but turn in and wait. Jason's a maniac about security. He has lots of incredible electronic devices."

"I'll bet," Bond said under his breath, but obeyed instructions, turning left and pushing the Mulsanne's snout to within an inch of the great high metal barriers. He would have put money on their being made of steel, worked to give the impression of wrought-iron ornamental bars. The gate-hangings themselves were shielded, behind massive stone pillars. There had to be some kind of closed-circuit television system, for the car sat waiting for only a matter of seconds before the locks clicked audibly, and the gates swung back.

As Bond had already divined, Endor was a large house. It had around twenty rooms. Classical Georgian in style, with a pillared porch and symmetrically placed sash windows like eyes peering out of the high golden stone, as though Endor itself watched the newcomers sliding gracefully up the drive. The crunch of gravel under the Bentley's wheels brought back many memories to him—the older cars he had once owned, and oddly, the books of Dornford Yates he'd read at school, with their adventurers riding forth to do battle in Bentleys or Rolls-Royce cars, usually to protect gorgeous ladies with very small feet.

Jason St. John-Finnes—Bond had learned to think of him by that name—stood by the open door, light shafting onto the turning circle. He had made no attempt at disguise. The decade in which he had been "dead" appeared to have taken no toll, for he looked exactly like the many photographs in his file at the Regent's Park Headquarters. Tall and slim, he was obviously in good physical condition, for he moved with grace and purpose. The famous green eyes were just as startling as Percy had maintained. By turns warm or cold, they were almost hypnotic, lively and penetrating, as though they could look deeply into a person's heart. The nose was indeed large and hooked—a great bill—so that the combination of bright searching eyes and the big sharp nose *did* give the impression of a bird of prey. Bond shuddered slightly. There was something exceptionally sinister about the scientist, but this unsettling facet all but vanished the moment he started to speak.

"Freddie!" He approached her with a kiss. "How splendid to see you, and I'm so glad to meet your friend." He stretched out a hand. "Bond, isn't it?"

The voice was low, pleasant, and full of laughter, the accent mid-Atlantic, almost Bostonian, the handshake firm, strong, warm and very friendly. It was as though a wave of good will and welcome passed through the flesh as their palms touched.

"Ah, here's Dazzle. Darling, this is Mr. Bond."

"James," he said, already in danger of being hypnotically charmed by the man. "James Bond."

For a few seconds his heart raced as he gazed at the tall, ash-blonde, slight-figured woman who had come out of the house. Then he realized that it was a trick of the light, for at a distance, especially as now at dusk, Dazzle could easily be taken for Percy Proud: the same hair, figure and bone structure, even the same movements.

Dazzle was as warm and welcoming as her husband. The pair of them had a curious effect, as though together they were able to enfold you, pulling you into some circle of enchantment. As they left the car and walked into the spacious hallway, Bond had the ridiculous desire to throw all caution to the wind and immediately face Jason, asking him what had really happened on that day so long ago when he had taken off on the ill-fated flight, what had been the purpose of disappearing, and what he was up to now.

During the whole of that evening, in fact, he had to keep a strong hold on himself not to come out into the open. Between them Jason and the vivacious Dazzle proved to be a daunting couple. Within minutes of being in their company one felt oneself an old friend. Jason, the story went, was Canadian by birth, while Dazzle came from New York, though you would have been hard put to place her accent, which had more of Knightsbridge in it and very little of Fifth Avenue.

The one matter never really discussed in detail during M's briefings had been finance, but now, seeing the house with its brilliant decor ("That's Dazzle," Jason laughed, "she has what the designers call flair") and obviously careful taste, one became aware of wealth. The large drawing room into which they were first taken was a clever blend of original Georgian and comfortable modern—the antique pieces counterpointing the quiet, striped wallpaper (a cream overlaid with lime) and not clashing with the more modern pictures, or the large buttoned-leather wing chairs and Chesterfields. Where, Bond wondered, did all this come from? Where were the (rich) bodies buried?

A Filipino houseboy appeared to serve the drinks, and the talk was almost exclusively about what a wonderful refurbishing job they had done on the house (that from Freddie) and amusing tidbits of local scandal.

"It's what I adore about life in a village," Jason gave a low chuckle. "My work doesn't allow for me to be what you might call socially active, but we still get all the gossip—because everybody does."

"Except the gossip about ourselves, darling," Dazzle said with a grin. Bond realized that her nose was similar to Percy's *before* it had been "bobbed."

There was an oddity. Was Jay Autem conscious of it? Bond wondered. Had he always known what the real Percy looked like?

"Oh, I get the gossip about us." Jason's voice was deep with humor. "Cindy and I are having a passionate love affair, while you're in bed most of the time with Peter Amadeus."

"Much good would it do me." Dazzle put a hand over her mouth, mockingly. "Where are they, anyway, dear? Peter and Cindy, I mean," she asked.

"Oh, they'll be up in a minute. They decided to play one more round of The Revolution. We've still got a good deal of preliminary work to do." He turned to Bond. "We're in the computer games business."

"So Freddie mentioned." At last he managed to break the spell, allowing a hint of superior disapproval into his tone.

Jason caught it at once. "Oh, but you're a computer programer as well, aren't you? Freddie told me."

"A little. Not games though. Not really." The stress on the word *games* was exact, designed to give the impression that the use of computers to play mere games was anathema to him.

"Aha," Jason wagged a finger, "but there are games and games, Mr. Bond. I'm talking about complex, highly original and undoubtedly intellectual

96

pastimes, not the whizz-bang-bang-shoot- 'em-up arcade rubbish. Who do you work for?"

Bond admitted he worked for nobody at the moment. "My training in programing was done when I worked for the Foreign Office," he said, trying to sound diffident.

"You're *that* Mr. Bond!" Dazzle sounded genuinely excited.

He nodded, "Yes, the notorious Mr. Bond. Also the innocent Mr. Bond."

"Of course." For the first time—like reality showing through a mask—there was a slightly dubious note to Jason's reply. "I read about your case."

"Were you really a spy?" Dazzle tended to become almost breathlessly excited by anything that interested her.

"I . . ." Bond began, then put on a show of floundering, so that Jason came to his rescue.

"I don't think that's the kind of question you're meant to ask, my dear." At that moment, Peter Amadeus and Cindy Chalmer came into the room.

"Ah, the amazing Doctor Amadeus," Jason rose.

"And Sinful Cindy," laughed Dazzle.

"I'd be flattered if they called *me* Sinful Freddie," said Lady Freddie as she greeted the pair.

"Sinful indeed!" Cindy was not black, as Freddie had told Bond, but more of a creamy coffee shade. "The product of a West Indian father and a Jewish

97

mother," she was later to confide in Bond, adding that there were a thousand racist jokes that could be made at her expense.

Dressed in a simple gray skirt and white silk shirt, Cindy had the figure and legs of a dancer, breasts like Ogen melons—the simile was ancient, but exact— and a face that reminded Bond of a very young Ella Fitzgerald. Peter, on the other hand, was around thirty—a few years older than Cindy—short, precise, prematurely balding and with a pedantic streak crossed with occasional glimpses of verbal viciousness that would have been the only hint of his sexual pre- dilection, had he not, as it turned out, been so bla- tantly honest about it.

After the introductions (Bond wondered if he imagined it, but Cindy Chalmer appeared to give him a long, almost conspiratorial, look), Dazzle suggested they go in to dinner. "Tomas'll be furious if his cook- ing is spoiled." Tomas was the near-invisible Filipino, and had learned to cook at the feet of Europe's great- est chefs—courtesy of Jason St. John-Finnes.

The meal was almost a banquet—a Lombardy soup, made from pouring boiling consommé over raw eggs sprinkled with Parmesan and laid on bread, partially fried in butter; smoked salmon mousse; ven- ison baked in a sauce of juniper berries, wine, chopped ham and lemons; and a dessert of pears in chocolate sauce, "Specially for Lady Freddie."

To begin with, the conversation mainly concerned the work that Cindy and Peter had just been doing.

"How did it go, then?" Jason asked as they sat down at a long refectory table set on bare polished boards in the dining room.

"We've found another couple of random problems you can set into the early section. Raise the general and search strengths of the British patrols, and you get some very interesting results." Peter gave a lopsided smile.

"And, to equalize, there's a new random for the later stages," Cindy added. "We've put in a random card that gives the colonial militia more uncaptured cannon. If you draw that option the British don't know the strength until they begin assaulting the hill."

Freddie and Dazzle were chattering away about clothes, but Jason caught Bond's interested eye. He turned to Peter and Cindy.

"Mr. Bond does not approve of using such high-tech magic for mere games," he said, smiling, and the comment was made with no malice.

"Ah, come on, Mr. Bond!"

"It's intellectual stimulation."

These remarks made by Cindy and Peter, in that order. Peter continued, "Is chess a frivolous use of wood, or ivory?"

"I said nothing of the kind." Bond laughed, knowing that the interrogation and testing time was getting close. "I was simply trained as a programer of Cobal and databases for government purposes . . ."

"Not military purposes, Mr. Bond?"

"Oh, the military use them, of course. I was a naval man, myself, but some time ago." He paused. "I was, in fact, intrigued. These games of yours—are they really games?"

"They are games in one sense," Peter answered. "I suppose they're also tutorials. We know that a lot of serving military people order our products."

"They teach, yes." Jason leaned over toward Bond. "You cannot sit down and play one of our games unless you have some knowledge of strategy, tactics and military history. They can be taxing—and they do require intelligence. It's a booming market, James." He paused, as though a thought had struck him. "What's the most significant leap forward in the computer arts—in your opinion, of course?"

Bond did not hesitate. "Oh, without doubt the advances being made, almost by the month, in the field of vastly increased storage of data, using smaller and smaller space."

Jason nodded. "Yes. Increased memory, in decreased space. Millions of accessible facts, stored for all time in something no larger than a postage stamp. And, as you say, it's increasing by the month, even by the day. In a year or so, the little home micro will be able to store almost as much information as the large mainframe computers used by banks and government departments. There is also the breakthrough that marries the laser video disk recording with computer commands—movements, actions, scale, response." They were already experimenting with such things, here. "At Endor we have a very sophisticated setup. You may like to look around after dinner."

"Put him on The Revolution and see if a novice player comes up with anything new," suggested Cindy.

"Why not?" The bright green eyes glittered, as though some challenge was in the offing.

"You've made a computer game out of what? The Russian Revolution?"

Jason laughed, "Not quite, James. You see, our games are vast—in a way too large for the home computer. They're all very detailed and require a great amount of memory to use. We pride ourselves on the playability, that area which makes the battles and campaigns 'fun' to fight, as well as being taxing, intellectually and mentally. We don't even like calling them games. Simulations is a better word. No, as yet we haven't got a simulation of any revolution. We are, though, preparing an interesting one of The American Revolution—you know, the final stages prior to the so-called War of Independence: Concord; Lexington; Bunker Hill. September 1774 to June 1775.

"At the moment, we have only six simulations on the market: Crécy, Blenheim, The Battle of the Pyramids—Napoleon's 1798 Egyptian expedition—Austerlitz, Cambrai, which is good, because the outcome could have been very different, and Stalingrad. We're very well advanced with one on the Blitzkrieg of 1940. And we're in the early stages of The American Revolution."

Bond remarked that Cindy and Peter talked as though they were actually playing the game—"I mean simulation," he hastily added.

"Freddie and I are going to look at dresses," Dazzle suddenly interrupted, rather sharply. "It's shop all the time. Very boring. See you later, James Bond."

Jason did not even apologize, merely smiling like a benign eagle. Freddie gave Bond a broad wink as the two ladies left the room, and, as he turned back to the table, he caught Cindy looking at him again, in the same almost conspiratorial way—tinged, this time, with jealousy. Or did he imagine it?

"Yes, to answer your query, James," Jason had hardly paused, "they *are* playing a kind of simulation. Naturally, you're conversant with flowcharting a computer program?"

Bond nodded, recalling the hours spent in Monaco. Once more, with the memory, came that odd sense of Percy's presence. He dragged himself back, for Jason had continued to speak.

"Before we prepare a detailed flowchart, we have to find out what we wish to chart. So we begin to discover the simulation by playing it on a large table. This acts as our graphics guide, and we have counters for units, troops, ships, cannon, plus cards for the random possibilities: weather cards, epidemics, unexpected gains or losses, hazards of war."

"From this," Peter took over, "we learn the scope of the program task. So, when we've played the campaign—"

"About a million times," Cindy added. "It seems like a million, anyway."

Peter nodded, "We're ready to begin flowcharting the various sections. You have to be dedicated in this job."

"Come," Jason's voice became commanding, "we will show James Bond the laboratory, and the board we're working on now. Who knows, he may become interested and return to battle it out with me. If you do," he looked straight at Bond, "make sure you have plenty of time. Campaigns cannot be fought in five minutes." Behind these seemingly pleasant words there was a hint of obsession, a glitter in the eyes that seemed to say that, somehow, the way of Jay Autem Holy led beyond reason.

As they left the room, Bond was conscious of Cindy brushing against him. He felt her hand touch lightly on his right hip, just where the ASP 9mm was holstered. Had that been accidental, or was she carrying out a subtle search? Whatever the answer, Cindy Chalmer, at least, knew that he was armed.

They went through the main hall, and Jason produced a bunch of keys attached to a thin gold chain. He unlocked a door that had once, he said, been the way down to the cellars. "We've made a few changes, naturally."

Naturally, Bond acknowledged, but was quite unprepared for the nature of the alterations. Below the house there were at least three large, well-equipped computer rooms, with several well-known makes of superior micros sitting in front of their Visual Display Units. But, in the last room—Jason's own office— Bond's heart leaped as he spotted a machine that was almost exactly, on the surface at least, like the Terror Twelve now safe in the Bentley's boot outside.

The walls of each room were filled with metal storage cabinets, and from his office Jason led the way into a long chamber, lit from above by at least thirty spotlights. Below them was a large table, while the walls were covered with charts and maps.

The table was overlaid with a thick plastic grid, below which rested a detailed map of the Eastern seaboard of America—centered on Boston—as it was in the 1770s. The main communicating roads and natural features were clearly marked in color, and the map took up almost the entire table.

In the center of the grid stood a rectangular framework made of black plastic, the size and shape of a large television screen, while two small easels had been placed at the far end, and a series of trays—on opposite sides of the table—contained packs of white three-by-five cards.

There were chairs placed so that players could sit in front of the trays, with desk tops to each player's right, replete with paper, maps and printed forms.

They began to explain the nature of the game, and how it was used to build up all the details of the simulation before anything was committed to a computer program.

The rectangular framework moved freely—though in a strict pattern—both vertically and horizontally across the map.

"That is the area a player will eventually see on his screen, when we have built the game." Jason's manner had become somehow less warm, as though the professional in him had suddenly ousted the friendly side of his nature. Now he explained how they could slot closeups of the terrain into the rectangle. "When we've got the game on computer, you'll be able to scroll around this whole map, but only see one section at a time," he said. "However, there's a zoom facility. You press the Z key, and the screen will give you a blowup of the section you've moved to."

Cindy explained that the two easels contained a calendar and the weather cards—each month's cards shuffled separately before play began. "Weather restricts or enhances movement." She demonstrated how the British patrols could move five spaces—arranged in hexagon shape—on good days, but in heavy rain only three, and in snow, two.

Looking at the map, Bond tried to remember the history of that period, learned too long ago in dusty schoolrooms. He thought of the frustration among officers of the colonial militia, of the British inability to protect the cities and towns; the unrest; then rebellion and open hostility.

Then there was a general—was it General Gage? —caught between his situation on the ground and the necessity to await orders from England. Of the patrols searching for the rebels' arms caches, the great warning ride of Paul Revere—which allowed the militia's weapons and ammunition to be moved out of Concord—and the skirmishes around that town and Lexington. All had finally led to a British withdrawal into Boston, dominated by the militia cannon on Bunker Hill. It was Bunker Hill that was remembered as a kind of Dunkirk by the Americans, for the British garrison had won the battle and taken the hill, but with such terrible losses that they had to retreat, by sea, to Halifax.

Bond thought of these things as Jason, warming to his theme, went on about the way the simulation was played. The players took turns in issuing orders, moving forces—some of the moves could be secret, and had to be noted on paper—then challenging and, possibly, skirmishing.

"The thing I find interesting is that you can alter

106

history. I am, personally, very attached to the idea of changing history." Again, the hint of obsession hovering just below the surface. The eyes glazed slightly, and the voice altered—a faraway, menacing sound. "Perhaps I *shall* alter history. A dream? Maybe, but dreams can turn into reality, if one man of brilliance is put to proper use. You think my spark of genius is put to proper use? No?" He expected no answer, and his next words really concerned something far and away beyond the game, or simulation. "Perhaps, James, we could look at this in more detail—even play a few sequences—say, tomorrow?"

Bond said he would like that, sensing more than an ordinary challenge. St. John-Finnes continued to talk of revolution, change and the complexity of war-games like this. Cindy made an excuse to leave, nodding at Bond and remarking that she hoped they would meet again.

"Oh, I'm certain you will," Jason appeared to be very sure of himself. "I'm inviting him to have another look, say, six tomorrow evening?"

Bond accepted, noticing that Jason did not even smile.

As they left, he walked on ahead, but Peter lingered to the rear, with Bond, taking the opportunity to whisper, "If you do play with him, he likes to win. Bad loser, and plays by the historical book. The poor dear always thinks his opponent will do exactly what was done in reality. Be warned. The man's a paradox." He gave Bond a wink that made it all too clear that Peter Amadeus was not particularly fond of his boss.

Upstairs, Dazzle awaited them. Cindy had gone to bed, and she had, herself, driven Freddie back to the Bull. "She seemed very tired. Said you had dragged her all around the countryside this afternoon, Mr. Bond. You really shouldn't subject her to so much physical exercise. She's very much a town mouse, you know."

Bond had his own thoughts about this. He also could do with a good night's sleep, but accepted the offer of a nightcap from his host. Peter and Dazzle made themselves scarce, leaving the two men alone.

After a short silence, Jason raised his drink.

"Tomorrow," he said, the green eyes like glass. "Maybe we won't play games, James. But I would welcome the chance of taking you on. Who knows? Computers, yes . . ." He was away again, in some world of his own with a different time, place and set of values. "Computers are either the greatest tool mankind has invented, the most magnificent magic, capable of destruction or the construction of a new age." He laughed, one sharp rising note. "Or they're the best toy God has provided." In a couple of seconds the more familiar Jason seemed to return, as though the tall commanding figure was inhabited by two spirits, one benign and one evil. "Can I share my thoughts about you, James?"

108

Throughout the evening, Bond had been conscious that the man who called himself Jason St. John-Finnes had been asking questions designed to entrap, and to lead the questioner into his subject's very soul.

"I think," Jason was not waiting for Bond's reply, or consent. "I think that you are a small fraud, Mr. Bond. That you know very little about the art of computer programing. Some, but not as much as you pretend. Am I right?"

"No." Bond was firm. "No, you're not right. I've had the standard courses that they give people like myself. I reckon that I'm adequate. Not in your class, though. But who is?"

"Plenty of people." Jason's voice was quiet. "Young Cindy, and Peter, to name two. It's a young people's profession, and future, James Bond. Yes, I have a lot of knowledge, and some flair for strategy. But young people who are brought up with the machines acquire flair very quickly. You know the age of the biggest, richest software tycoon in the United States?"

"Twenty-eight."

"Right. Twenty-eight years of age, and some of the really advanced programers are younger. I know it all, but it's up to people like Cindy, or Peter, to translate the agility of my ideas into reality. Brilliance, genius, requires nurturing. Programers like my two may not really know that they feed my great conceptions. As for you, a man with minimal training—

you cannot be of real use to me. You don't stand a chance in this field."

Bond shrugged. "Not against you," he said, not understanding if this was some devious wordplay, some psychological ploy.

At the door, Jason told him he looked forward to the next meeting. "If you feel you can take me on—at a game I mean—I'll be happy to oblige. But, maybe, we'll find something more interesting than games, eh? Six tomorrow."

Bond was not to know how the game of life itself would have changed by the time he saw Jay Autem Holy again. Nor what was really at stake in the games this tall, unhinged man liked to play. He did know that Holy was a man possessed, a dangerous, possibly psychotic case. Beneath the bonhomie and charm, he thought, lay the mind of one who would play God with the world, and he found this deeply disturbing.

The renovations at the Bull were very much in keeping with the inn's original style, so no modern knob-locks or cards had been fitted to the bedroom doors. Just good old-fashioned mortise locks. Bond retrieved his large key from a dozing night porter and went up to his room. But, on putting the key in his lock, he found the door already open. Freddie, he thought, with some irritation, for he wanted very much to have time in which to think.

He remained cautious, slipping the automatic pistol from its holster, holding it just behind his right thigh, turning the handle and gently kicking the door open.

"Hallo, Mr. Bond." Cindy Chalmer smiled up at him from one of the chairs, her long legs sprawled out in front of her, like an invitation.

Quietly, Bond closed the door.

"I bring greetings from Percy," Cindy's smile broadened into a bewitching grin.

Bond remembered the looks she had given him during the evening. "Who's Percy?" he asked evenly, holding her eyes with his, trying to detect either truth or deception.

– 9 –

Endor Games

"COME ON, MR. BOND. Percy Proud. Persephone. We're in cahoots."

"Sorry, Cindy. Nice of you to drop by, but I've never heard of Percy, Persephone, or Proud." He quietly slipped the automatic pistol back into its holster. Cindy would have to do better than this, if he was going to accept her. Face value and a mention of Percy was not enough.

We've even infiltrated Endor, he heard Percy whisper into the echo chamber of his mind.

"You're very good." Cindy spoke like a cheeky schoolgirl. "Percy said you were. She also told me that I had to mention you liked treats, and an apple for the teacher always brought great rewards."

Bond remained cautious. Certainly only Percy and he knew about his byplay with the apple—in Monte Carlo—and their jokes concerning rewards for pupils. But . . . ? "You're in cahoots—as you put it—with someone called Percy?" he went on, staring her out.

Cindy bobbed her head, teeth like an advertisement against the cream coffee of her face. "Cahoots; intrigue; in league with. We both belong to the same outfit, Mr. Bond."

It made some sense. If the American Service already had someone in the house, close to Jay Autem Holy, they would not broadcast the fact. Persephone, as a true professional, would not tell Bond either. The circle of knowledge would be confined until the last minute. So, was this the last minute?

"Tell me more."

"She said—Percy said—you'd know what to do with these." The girl produced two hard disks from her shoulder bag. They were encased in plastic, making thin square boxes a little over five inches to a side and less than a quarter of an inch deep. On one side of the square there was a hinged flap, like those on much fatter video cassettes. The square wafers were both colored in brilliant blue and had small labels stuck on one corner.

He made no move to even touch them. "And what, Miss Chalmer, are those?"

"A couple of our target's less conventional pro-

114

grams. And I can't hang on to them for long. At about four in the morning I turn into a pumpkin."

"I'll get a couple of white mice to drive you home, then."

"Seriously. I can manage to get past the security without being detected, until about four. They change shifts then."

"We're talking of getting back into Endor, I take it?"

"Of course we're talking about Endor. The place is electronically buttoned like Fort Knox—you remember Fort Knox?" A small, almost mocking smile. "Well, Endor has code and lock combinations that change with each security shift. I have to go back during the current phase. Otherwise I'll be right up the proverbial tributary without oars, as they say."

Bond asked if she did this often.

"In the mating season, yes. That's why I've cultivated a certain reputation in the village. So's I have a kind of alibi if I ever get caught. But, if they cop me with these stuffed down my shirt . . . Well." She ran a finger over her throat. "So, Mr. Bond, I'd appreciate it if you'd copy these little beauties."

"How unconventional are they?" He reached out to take the disks, feeling as though something irrevocable could happen once he laid hands on them. To actually handle the things implied that he *could* do as Cindy asked. If, though, this was an attempt to frame him, there would be no going back.

"You'll see. But please do what has to be done as quickly as you can. I have no way of copying them at the house . . ."

"You can borrow them, but not make copies? I find that difficult to believe, Miss Chalmer. Your boss told me, not long ago, that you're a wizard with these things."

She made an irritated, spluttering noise that inexplicably reminded him of M, when the Head of Service became annoyed. "Technically, of course I can copy. But in fact, it would be exceptionally dangerous to try it in the house. I'm never left alone with the essential hardware for very long at one time. Either the great man's around, or the Queen of the Night is fussing about . . ."

"The who?"

"Queen of . . . Oh, Peter. That's my pet name for him. I think he may well be quite trustworthy—he certainly loathes the boss—but it's not worth the risk. Percy wouldn't hear of it."

Bond smiled inwardly.

She raised her eyes, indicating a ready response for any question.

"How well do you know this Percy?"

"You're dreadfully coy, James." They now slipped easily into first-name terms.

"No, I'm dreadfully careful."

"I know her quite well. Have done for the past, what? Eight years?"

"Has she been hospitalized since you've known her? Medical operations of any kind?"

"A nose job. Spectacular. That's all."

"And you?"

"I've never had a nose job."

"Background, Cindy. What? Who? And why?"

"All of it? Okay. I spent eight months in a hospital for infectious diseases after I left high school. There are medical records, doctors and nurses who remember me. I know because Old Bald Eagle's ferrets checked them out. Only I wasn't there. I was at the Farm, being trained. Then, surprise, I won a scholarship to Cambridge University, England. From then on, as pure as the proverbial driven. A good, hardworking girl. I'm untouchable, fully sanitized, as we say. The Company kept me on ice. I worked for IBM and with Apple before I applied for the job with Jay Autem Holy, and his boys checked, double-checked and then didn't trust me for eighteen months."

Bond gave a brisk nod. There were no real options left. Trust, between him and the girl, had to be entered into quickly, though not lightly. "Okay, just tell me about these two programs."

"Why don't you take a look for yourself? Percy gave me to understand you had the means."

"Tell me, Cindy. Concisely as you can, then we'll get on with it."

She talked rapidly, reducing the information, telescoping her sentences to the minimum. They had

games weekends at Endor—he knew about that—
and some very strange people turned up along with
the usual dedicated wargames freaks. "There are two
particular characters—Balmer and Hopcraft."

"Tigerbalm and Happy, yes." M had briefed him
on this pair, nicknames included.

"Tigerbalm's about as balmy as a force ten blizzard. Kill you quick as look at you; and Happy's probably only that way when he's raping or pillaging.
Happy would've made a good Viking raider."

The Gunfire Weekends, as they were called in the
computer magazines, all appeared to be run with a military flavor—"Strict discipline. Order Groups at 0900
hours. Lights out at 2230, and all that." It was what
happened after lights out that became interesting.

"The oddballs are detailed to rooms near one another, and always near Tigerbalm and Happy. The
weekends cover three nights. The oddballs all leave
looking as though they've been awake for a week. In
fact they get very little sleep, because, around midnight—on each night—they're down in Old Bald Eagle's private den, behind the filing cabinets in the War
Room, where we looked at The Revolution plotter.

"And there they stay, all night, working on their
own little games, two of which I'd like to get back into
their files before the dawn's early light."

Bond told her to wait in his room while he went
quietly down to the car, selected the equipment he
required, and brought it back to the room.

"For God's sake." Cindy looked at the Terror Twelve with undisguised pleasure. "She certainly got it right. I only hope the circuit diagrams I provided are accurate."

He'd buy that: Cindy monitoring the technology advance at Endor to provide Percy with all the ammunition required to build a computer identical to the one Holy had devised over the years. It also provided another motivation for Bond's infiltration. Maybe he was there only to get the latest programs out. After that, others could step in and clean out the stables, armed with evidence provided by himself, Percy and Cindy. Who knew?

With the console, and hard laser drives plugged in, Bond took the first disk and booted up. The moment the first menu of options came onto the screen he knew what it was about: in a series of flashing colored letters on the television screen, the menu read:

Phase One—Airport to Ken High Street
    A. First Girl Driver.
    B. Second Girl Driver.
    C. Advance Car.
    D. Trail Taxi.

He accessed the First Girl Driver and the screen showed him to be in heavy traffic, inbound from Heathrow Airport. Ahead lay the small convoy of police and security vans. The program was obvious, and Bond flipped through the phases—Turn Off; Kensington High Street: Phase One; Kensington High Street: Phase Two; Abort; Kensington High Street: Phase Violet Smoke, and on to Getaway, passing things like Security Teams (Electrics) and Security Teams (Way Out). He did not need to run the whole simulation to know that the disk currently resting in his top drive was a training program for the Kruxator Collection robbery—that superbly planned heist which had taken place on the day of his own setup Press conference.

Taking a virgin disk, Bond began to go through the careful procedure of breaking down Jay Autem Holy's protection program in order to make a clean second copy of the original.

The process was slow, for Holy had used not only the regular, easy system of "scribbling" on some sectors of the disk, but also the small "routine" Percy had shown to Bond. In effect this was a program in itself, designed to "crash" the disk, making it completely useless if anyone even attempted to copy it. Following Percy's tuition, he was now able to, first, detect the program, and then remove it, line by line, before matching up his virgin disk so that it would be in a format to exactly copy the original. The work took over an hour, but at the end there was a true clone of Holy's training program for the Kruxator robbery. A further twenty minutes was spent in returning the protect program to the original disk.

The second of Cindy's disks was, as they found very quickly, a similar training program—this time, they presumed, for the hijacking of an aircraft. As there had been a monumental hijacking of an especially chartered freight plane, carrying newly printed money from the Royal Mint printers to several countries, the chances were that this was the blueprint for that particular piece of villainy.

Once more, the cloning process began, but this time with more urgency, for Cindy had become anxious about her return.

"There is one other thing." She looked tired and concerned.

Without taking his eyes off the screen, Bond grunted a "Yes?"

"Something very big's going on. Not a robbery, I'm pretty sure of that, but a criminal—probably violent—operation. There've been callers in the night, and I've heard several references to a special program."

"What kind of special program?"

"I've heard the name only—they call it The Balloon Game, and there seem to be specialists involved."

Bond was concentrating, writing back the protect program onto the hijack simulation original. "They're all specialists, Cindy. Even Tigerbalm's a specialist."

"No, I've seen some of these guys. Oh, certainly some of them are hoods and heavies; but others are like pilots and parsons."

"Parsons?"

"Well, not exactly. Doctors and dentists, if you like. Upright. Professional."

"The Balloon Game?"

"I heard Tigerbalm use the expression, and one of the others—talking to the Holy Terror. Will you report it, please, I think it's something nasty."

Bond said he would be getting the copies of these two programs to London with speed. He'd mention The Balloon Game at the same time. "You think they're using it now? Training on it?"

"Positive."

"If we could get a copy . . ."

"Not a chance. Not yet, anyway."

He fell silent, finishing off the job in hand. Presently he rattled off a description of Rolling Joe Zwingli. "Ever see anyone like him around Endor?" He asked.

"General Zwingli? I recognize the description, and the answer's no. I had some garbled message from Percy that he's alive." She paused, adding that this seemed incredible.

"Stranger than fiction." Bond completed his tasks and started to close things down, returning the original disks to Cindy, asking, finally, about the routine at the house—did Jason and Dazzle ever go out? Or away? How many security people did they have around?

She usually referred to Jay Autem as the target, or Old Bald Eagle. Yes, he went away for a couple of days or so about once a month—always left, and returned, at night. Never left the house during the day; never showed his face in the village. "Very cagy, our target. Dazzle's out and about a great deal—the village, Oxford, London and trips abroad. I suspect she's really the liaison officer."

"Where abroad?"

"Middle East. Europe. All over. Percy's got the list. I try to keep track—mainly from hotel book matches, or flight labels. But she's cagy as well. Gets rid of a lot of stuff before she comes home."

As for the household, there was one Filipino boy and four security men. "He has six genuine sales reps who wouldn't suspect anything. But they're on the outside. The four security blokes double as reps and staff. It's very good cover. Would've had me fooled if I hadn't known better. They're all quiet, efficient guys—two cars between them; out and about a great deal; managing the telephones, taking orders, distributing the genuine Gunfire Simulations packages. But two of them never leave the house. They work on a strict rota, and the electronics are highly sophisticated. Breakable, but clever. I mean you have to know the system to fiddle it. What's more, as I've already told you, they alter the codings for every shift. You can only get in and out if you know the numbers for a particular six-hour period; and, even then, the machines have to know your voice-print."

"Visual?" Bond asked.

"Quite a lot—the main gates, large areas of the walls, front and rear of the house. You can only dodge the closed-circuit visual stuff at the back, and then only if you know the pattern: they change that with the lock codings, so you really do need to know each six-hour period to get in, or out, without being detected. An intruder wouldn't last three minutes."

"Ever had any?"

"Intruders? Only a tramp, and one false alarm— at least they presume it was a false alarm."

"Weapons?"

"I was around when the false alarm was triggered. Yes, one of the guys on duty had a hand gun. So I've seen one. There're probably more. James, can I get going? I can't afford to get caught with these disks on me. There are blank fakes in the cabinets, and they rarely get taken out. But if I . . ."

"On your way, Cindy, and good luck. I'll see you tonight. The little tournament I'm fighting against our target. By the way, your friend Peter tipped me off about Jason's style of play . . ."

"He doesn't like to lose," she grinned. "Almost pathological, like a child. It's a matter of honor with him."

Bond did not smile. "And me," he said softly. "It's a matter of honor with me."

It was past three-thirty in the morning. Bond packed up the equipment and took it down to the car, locking it away in the boot but leaving the cloned programs in a FloppiPak disk mailer, wryly contemptuous of the revolting nomenclature of trade items such as this.

Addressing the label to himself, at one of the "convenience" box numbers, he weighed the small, flat package in his hand, making an intelligent guess before taking a folder of postage stamps from his briefcase. He wanted to deliver the package in person, but was not going to leave anything to chance.

Sitting at the small dressing table, Bond next wrote a short note, on hotel paper, to Freddie.

Gone to Oxford for the morning. Didn't want to wake you, but will be back for lunch. How about a return match this afternoon?
—J.

Stripping off, he ran a cold shower and stepped under it, holding his face against the stinging needle spray, and gasping at the initial shock. After a minute or so, he added some warm water, soaped himself, then rubbed down, toweling his body with brisk, tingling ruthlessness before shaving and climbing into his underwear, a pair of black Ted Lapidus cords, and a black cotton rollneck. Then he strapped the ASP automatic in its holster so that it lay hard against his right hip, before putting on a light suede jacket and pushing his feet into the old favorite moccasins.

It was just getting light, the darkness changing to gray, and then that pearl, cold-washed sky which heralded unsettled weather.

With the detested FloppiPak in his briefcase, Bond went downstairs, left his key and the note for Freddie at a deserted Reception, and went out to the car.

The Bentley's engine growled into life at the first turn of the key, and he allowed it to settle to its normal, gentle purr, fastening the seatbelt and watching the red warning lights flick off one by one.

Releasing the foot brake, he slid the selector into drive and let the car roll forward. If he took the Oxford road, turned onto the Ring Road, and then headed for the M40, he could be in London within ninety minutes.

It began to rain as he reached the big roundabout on the periphery of the Ring Road, taking the dual freeway, heading toward London. He was a mile or so along this stretch when the gray Mercedes of the day before appeared in his mirror.

Bond cursed silently, tightened his seatbelt and eased his foot down on the accelerator. The car slid forward, gathering power, the speedometer rising to 100, then 120.

There was little traffic as yet, and he slid neatly in and out among the stray cars and lorries, mainly keeping to the fast lane.

The Mercedes held back, but, even at speed, Bond could not throw him. Ahead the signs came up for an exit, and, flicking the indicator at the last moment, he left the dual carriageway still well in excess of the 100 mph mark, the Bentley responding to his fingertips, holding the road tightly in the turn.

The Mercedes seemed to have disappeared. He hoped that the driver had not been able to reduce speed in time to get off the main two-lane highway. Ahead, the road narrowed, fir trees shadowing either side, and a lumbering heavy transporter grumbling along at fifty behind a petrol tanker.

The Bentley's speed dropped off, and, as he rounded the next bend, Bond caught a flash of headlights, blinking on and off from a layby. The next time he looked there was another Mercedes—white—hooking itself onto his tail.

Radio contact, he thought, and probably five or six cars covering him. Taking the next left, he picked up the telephone and, without allowing his eyes to leave the road, punched out the numbers that would access the duty officer, on a scrambled radio line, at the Regent's Park Headquarters.

The road narrowed and the second Mercedes was still there as he negotiated the next turn and the DO answered.

"Gamesman flash for Dungeonmaster," Bond spoke rapidly. "Am being followed, south of Oxford. Important package for Dungeonmaster. Will attempt mail. Addressed myself. The Programer is definitely involved all illegal actions as thought. Investigate Balloon Game. Speak to the Goddess." He was Gamesman; M the Dungeonmaster; Jay Autem Holy the Programer; while, naturally, Persephone Proud had been cryptoed Goddess.

"Understood," the duty officer said, and the line was closed. As he took the next bend, Bond realized he had outdistanced the Mercedes, and there was a village coming up. He pumped the big central foot-brake, slowing dramatically, looking ahead and to the left.

The car was almost out of the village before he spotted it—the welcome brilliant red of a post box. The Bentley slid to a halt beside the box, and Bond had the straps off before the car stopped rolling.

It took less than twenty seconds to slip the package into the open maw of the box and return to the driving seat. This time he did not rebuckle the belt until later, rolling the Bentley out and gathering speed as the Mercedes came into view again.

He passed an electric milk float, doing the early rounds, and held the left-hand bend, which took him into open country, then through trees again. As he reached the trees, Bond caught a glimpse of a picnic area sign, then saw the other two cars emerge from the trees, their bonnets coming together to form a V, blocking his path.

"Playing for keeps," he muttered, ramming the footbrake and hauling on the wheel with his left arm.

As the Bentley began to slew, broadside on, he was conscious of the white Mercedes, now close behind him.

The speedometer was touching sixty as the Bentley left the road, plunging among the trees, over bracken, zigzagging wildly and trying to negotiate a path that would bring him back to the road.

The first bullet made a grating, gouging sound on the roof, and Bond could only think of the damage it would do to the coachwork. The second hit his rear offside tire, sending over five thousand pounds weight of custom-built motor car side on into a tangle of bushes.

Slammed against the seatbelt, Bond reached simultaneously for the 9mm automatic pistol and the electric window button.

– 10 –

Erewhon

THE ASP 9mm is a small, very lethal weapon. Essentially a scaled-down version of the Smith & Wesson Model 39, the ASP has been in use with United States Intelligence agencies for more than a decade. With a recoil no greater than that of a Walther .22, it has the look of a target automatic rather than the deadly customized hand gun it really is, for Armaments Systems and Procedures—the organization that carried out the conversion—produced the weapon to exacting specifications: concealability; a minimum eight-round capacity; reliability; an ammunition indicator, by way of Lexon see-through butt grips; and an acceptance of all known 9mm ammunition.

The rounds in Bond's magazine were particularly unpleasant: Glaser Safety Slugs. A Glaser is a prefragmented bullet that contains several hundred Number 12 shot, suspended in liquid Teflon. The velocity of these slugs, from the ASP, is over seventeen hundred feet per second; they will penetrate body armor before blowing, and a hit from a Glaser—on any vital area of the body—is usually fatal.

He fired two rounds from the lowered window almost before the car had come to a halt—both eyes open and looking down the revolutionary Guttersnipe sight, back-mounted, with three triangular yellow walls that give instant target acquisition.

Through the bushes, trees and bracken, men were visible around the cars—waving, gunning motors to get the vehicles off the road, while others clambered toward the Bentley. Bond's rapid shots were aimed at the clear outline of a tall man, wearing a dirty-white raincoat, but he did not stop to find out what happened to the target. Jerking open the door, he rolled from the car, low into the undergrowth.

Branches seemed to clutch and scratch at him, but Bond continued to roll, determined to get as far away as possible from the Mulsanne Turbo.

He moved to the right, putting about twenty yards distance between himself and the car in less than sixty seconds. He twisted, flat on his belly, gun up and ready, eyes constantly moving—left, right, center— covering a wide sweeping sightline.

132

The cars had been backed off the road, and he guessed they now simply contained drivers. Only two figures were visible, but, almost by intuition, he reckoned there had to be at least four others fanning out, moving low and trying to encircle him.

Bond lay quite still, allowing his breathing to settle and his body to adjust in the undergrowth as he assessed the situation.

If they were methodical—and he had no reason to doubt it—these men would eventually find him: It was even possible they might call up reserves. Certainly there had to be more men available. How else could they have been certain of picking him up on the road, unless the Bentley had a location homer stuck onto it?

They would, Bond reasoned, find him later, rather than sooner. There should be time for him to coordinate a plan and make good his escape. Who were they? he found himself asking—some of Jay Autem Holy's hoods? There had to be a connection, but Holy—or St. John-Finnes—would have had ample opportunity to get him dead to rights that evening, at Endor. Unless . . . ? Unless . . . ? There were two possibilities—either Cindy had set him up, or Cindy, herself, had been caught. If the latter, a watch on him had been activated with great speed. Another "unless"—unless he had been under close surveillance from the word go, and Bond did not think that was on. He was operational and rarely left things to chance. The surveillance team would have to be very good indeed, and, apart from the obvious Mercedes—and Freddie's Jaguar—yesterday—he was ninety-eight percent certain that there had been no large team locked on to him.

It was now raining quite hard. One could hear the steady pattering from the branches, and the hiss coming from tires on the road. There was some shelter in this stretch of woodland, but, if the rain kept up, the day would become soggy.

To attempt a move now would be suicidal. He was at least one hundred and fifty yards from the road, and even if he reached the cars without being intercepted—which was unlikely—he would still be outnumbered three to one. Wait, he told himself. Patience. He must try to follow their search, and make sure nobody bounced him from behind.

He continued to watch the arc to his front, gently turning his head to look to the rear when he reached far left and far right, straining his ears to catch any sound or word.

There was silence now that the cars were off the road, as though, by a prearranged signal, the pursuers had reverted to hand signals. The two men originally visible to his front had disappeared, while the sounds of movement would now be successfully blotted out by the audible rain.

The minutes ticked by, and, from his own reckoning, Bond had been lying in cover for the best part of fifteen minutes before he got a positive fix on any of them. The sharp crack of a branch and a flicker of movement on the far left caught ear and eye at the same moment. With tediously careful slowness he swiveled his neck. There, not more than twenty paces away, a man crouched against a tree, looking to the right of where Bond lay.

From his attitude, the compact alert manner, the way he kept low, using the bottom of the tree trunk for cover, and the small revolver, steady in the right hand held against left shoulder, the man signaled professionalism—a man well trained, a soldier of one kind or another. He was also searching in the calm, cautious manner of a hunter—eyes not just moving around, but methodically examining every square foot of ground within a specified arc.

That meant there was probably another like him to his left, or right, or both. What was more, it could only be a matter of time before his eyes came to rest on the ground where Bond lay.

The searcher appeared to be olive-skinned. His complexion seemed to match the denim trousers, shirt and military jacket he wore. Moving each limb about half an inch at a time, Bond began to turn. If need be he wanted to at least get a shot in before anyone else closed on him.

Another stir—this time on the right—caused Bond to change pace, his reflexes and intuition warning of danger, the ASP coming up in the direction of this new threat.

The triple, three-dimensional yellow walls that angle to form the Guttersnipe sight fell automatically into their correct triangular patterns, right on target—another figure, running, low between the trees, and much too close for any real comfort.

In the wink of an eye, Bond's brain instructed his muscles, fingers, eyes and reflexes to deal with both men, roll to the left and then check for a third, and maybe fourth, target. He was conscious of the first man bringing his revolver up in a two-handed grip, then—

The unmistakable click of a revolver hammer being drawn back, very close behind him, and the sharp burning cold of a muzzle placed gently on the side of his neck.

"Drop it, Mr. Bond. Please don't try to be silly. Just drop the gun."

Bravery was one thing; sheer recklessness another. Bond had no desire to get himself killed at this point in his career. He tossed the ASP onto the ground in front of him.

"Good." The voice was unfamiliar, soft, slightly lilting. "Now, hands on the head, please."

The two who had caused Bond to move too late were now standing, coming forward, the one to his left with arms outstretched, holding a snub-nosed revolver in the two-handed grip, the arms steady as iron bars, his eyes never leaving their captive. Bond was in no doubt that two bullets would reach him fast if he made any wrong move.

The other came in quickly, scooping up the fallen ASP like a predatory bird swooping onto its prey.

"Right, now get to your feet very slowly," the voice continued, the gun muzzle detaching itself from just behind Bond's ear. There was the sound of feet shuffling as the unseen man stepped back. "That maneuver is rather good, isn't it? We knew the rough area where you had gone to ground, so it was merely a matter of showing you someone with stealth, and another with speed. The lads went through that little farce three times before they found the right place. It's the kind of fieldcraft we teach. Please turn around."

"Who teaches?" He turned, and found himself facing a tall, well-built man in his mid-thirties—tight curly hair, dark above jet eyes, a square face, large nose and full lips. For all that, women would find him attractive, Bond thought. The complexion was overlaid with a hard, sunbaked tan, with which he could well have been born. It was the eyes that really gave him away, for they had that particular look, as if, for years, they had searched horizons for the telltale sign of dust; or the sky for a speck that could easily turn itself into a shrieking dive of death; or outcroppings of rock, for movement—even doorways and windows, the muzzle flashes. Those eyes had probably been doing that kind of thing since childhood. Nationality? Who could tell? One of the Middle Eastern countries obviously, but whether he came from Jerusalem, Beirut or Cairo was impossible to tell.

"Who teaches?" He asked again, and the young man lifted an eyebrow. "You may get to find out, Mr. Bond. Who knows?" The smile was not unfriendly. "Now," he said, "we have to move you, and I cannot be certain you'll sit still." He gave a short laugh, "I rather think my superiors want you alive and in one piece, so could you take off your jacket and roll up your sleeve?"

One of the other men had come into view—the one Bond had first spotted, and whom he now thought of as the Shootist, for he was obviously a very careful fighter with a hand gun. Two more figures rose from the bushes, as the senior man holstered his own weapon, reaching into a hip pocket to bring out a hard oblong box.

One of the newcomers helped to remove Bond's jacket while the other's hands rested firmly on his shoulders. Unresisting, Bond allowed them to roll up his sleeve while the leader, with great professionalism, filled a hypodermic syringe, lifting it so that the needle pointed upward. A tiny squirt of colorless liquid arced into the air.

Bond felt a damp swab on the upper part of his arm.

"It's okay," the leader smiled again. "We do want

you in one piece, I assure you." The smile broadened. "As the actress said to the bishop, just a little . . . er . . . a little jab."

One of the men laughed aloud, and Bond heard another say something in a language he did not recognize. He did not even feel the needle slide home, only saw the mist creeping up around the trees to envelop him. Cloud—damp, gray and clammy. Then darkness.

At first he thought he was in a helicopter, lying flat on his back while the machine bucked under him. He could hear the chug of the engine turning the rotor blades. Then, far away, the rip of automatic fire.

For a time, Bond drifted away again, then the helicopter sensation returned, and he realized that his consciousness had been cut into by a series of loud explosions near at hand.

Opening his eyes, he saw the fan, turning slowly on its electric motor above his head. The fan, white walls, a simple metal bedframe on which he lay, fully dressed.

He propped himself on one elbow to take stock. No ill effects. Physically he felt fine: no nausea, no headache, eyes focused properly. He held out his right hand, fingers splayed—not a tremor.

The fan kept turning, and he looked around the room. Nothing. Just the bed. No furniture. Nothing on the walls. One door, a window covered with bars and steel mesh on the outside, and another kind of mesh inside. Sunlight forced its way through the aperture, and as he swung his feet onto the floor there was another explosion—a dull, double crump, at a distance, so that the room did not even shudder at the force.

He stood up and still felt normal. Halfway to the door, there was the brip of machine-gun fire—again at a distance. The door was, of course, locked, and he could make out little through the window. The mesh on the inside was a thick papery adhesive substance that had been applied to the panes of glass, making it impossible to get any clear view. It would also prevent fragmentation from blast. Bond was convinced of two things. He was certainly not in England. The warmth inside the little white room, even with the fan phutting round and round, was not induced by the kind of heat you ever got in England, even during the most brilliant of summers. Also, the sounds of small arms fire, punctuated by the occasional explosion, made it appear likely that he was in some war zone.

He tried the door again, then had a look at the lock. No way. It was solid, well-made, and more than efficient.

Methodically he went through his pockets. Nothing. They had cleaned him out. Even his watch was missing, and the metal bedframe appeared to be a one-piece affair. Given time, and some kind of lever, he might well force a piece of thick wire from the springs. But it would be an arduous business, and—whoever they were—it was not in the cards that he would be left alone for long at a stretch.

When in doubt, do nothing.

He went back to the bed and stretched out, going back, in his mind, over the events still fresh on the track of his memory.

The attempt to get away with the computer programs. Posting them. The trailing cars. The wood and his capture. The needle. He was the only one to have fired a shot. Almost certainly he had hit—probably killed—one of them. Yet apart from their natural caution, they had been careful to make sure that he was unharmed.

Conclusions? None. A connection between his visit to Jay Autem Holy and the current situation was probable, though not absolutely certain. Take nothing for granted. Wait for revelations. Expect the worst.

Bond lay there, mentally prepared, for the best part of twenty minutes. At last there were footsteps, muffled, as though boots crunched over earth, but the tread still retained a military flavor. Bolts were drawn back.

As the door opened, he caught a glimpse of sand, low white buildings, and two armed men, dressed in olive-drab uniforms. A third person stepped into the room. He was the one who had administered the knockout injection in the Oxfordshire wood. Now he wore a uniform—simple olive-drab battledress; no insignia or badges of rank; desert boots; a revolver, of high caliber, holstered on the right of his webbing belt; a long sheathed knife on the left. His head was covered by a light brown, almost makeshift, *kaffiyeh* held with an Apache-type red band.

One of the men outside reached in and closed the door.

"Have a good sleep, Mr. Bond?" The man's smile was almost infectious. As he looked up, Bond remembered his feelings about the eyes.

"I'd rather have been awake." Give nothing until you were given; share nothing; accept nothing.

"You're all right, though? No ill effects?"

Bond shook his head.

"Right." Crisp, businesslike. "My name's Simon." An extended hand, which Bond did not take.

A slight pause, then: "We hold no grudge concerning our man. You killed him, by the way. But he was being paid to risk his life." Simon shrugged. "We underestimated you, I fear. My fault. Nobody thought you'd be carrying. After all, you're not in the trade any more. I reasoned that, if you were armed, it would be for old time's sake, and nothing as lethal as that thing. It's unfamiliar to us, incidentally. What is it exactly?"

"My name is James Bond, formerly Commander,

142

Royal Navy. Number CH 4539876. Formerly Foreign
Service. Now retired."

Simon's face creased into a puzzled look for a couple of seconds, then cleared. "Oh yes. I see. Name,
rank and number." He gave a one-note laugh. "Sorry
to disappoint you, Commander Bond, but you're not
a prisoner of war. When you outran us in that beautiful motor car there was no way to let you know we
came as emissaries. Friendship. A possible job."

"You could have shouted. In the wood, you could
have shouted, if that was the truth."

"And would you have believed us?"

Silence.

"Quite. No, I think not, Commander Bond. So we
took action to bring you in alive and well, using only
minimal force."

Bond thought for a moment. "I demand to know
where I am, and who you people are."

"In good time. All in—"

"Where am I?" He snapped.

"In Erewhon." Simon gave a low chuckle. "Like so
many organizations that don't wish to come under
public scrutiny, we go in for atrocious code names,
cryptonyms. For safety, security and our peace of
mind—just in case you turn down the job; or even
prove to be not quite the man we require—this place
is called Erewhon." His smile switched on and off,

wry and humorless as he added, "Now sir, the officer commanding would like a word."

Bond slowly got off the bed, reaching out a restraining arm, clasping his hand around Simon's left wrist, and aware of the man's other hand drifting very quickly to the revolver butt. "Commander, I wouldn't advise . . ."

"Okay," Bond said, releasing Simon's wrist. "I just don't recall having applied for a job. Not with anybody."

"Oh, really? No, I suppose you haven't." There was mocking disingenuousness in Simon's voice. "But you're out of work, Commander Bond. That's true, surely?"

"Yes."

"And, by nature, you're not an idle man. We wanted to—how would you say it? We wanted to put something your way." The on-off smile again. "That's why the officer commanding Erewhon wishes to talk to you."

Bond appeared to think for a moment, then he nodded. "I'll see your OC, then."

"Good." Simon rapped on the door, and one of the men outside opened up.

As they stepped outside, the two guards took station on either side. Bond sniffed the air. It was warm, but clear. Rare. They were fairly high above sea level, that was plain. They were also in a small depression, the flat bed of a hollow surrounded by hills. On one side the hills were low—a curving double mound, like a woman's breasts, but pitted with rock among the dry, sandy earth. The rest of the circle was more forbidding, crests and peaks running up several hundred feet, with ragged outcrops of unforgiving rock. The sun was high, almost directly above them, and along the flat sand bottom of the hollow were ranged a series of low white buildings laid out in one long rank, with divisions, and another terrace with three out-strokes, like a large letter E. Away, hard under the high ground there were other, similarly built structures: planned, but not regimented. Simon led them across the five or six hundred yards toward one of these latter blocks.

As they went, Bond kept his eyes alert. Smoke drifted up from some of the smaller buildings. To his left there was a firing range, with a group of uniformed people preparing to use it. Back, toward the hills, a clutter of gutted brick houses—looking almost European—suddenly erupted to the sound of heavy explosions and small arms fire. Figures dashed between these houses as though fighting a street battle, flashes among the smoke as grenades exploded.

As he turned at the noise, Bond also caught sight of some kind of bunker dug into the rock toward the top of one of the hills. A great defensive position, he thought. Easy to defend and almost impossible to attack by air, though helicopter-borne landings would, presumably, be possible.

"You like our Erewhon?" Simon asked cheerfully.

"Depends what you do here. Do you run package tours?"

Simon's forehead lifted, "Almost." He sounded quite amused.

They reached the building—about the size of a modest bungalow. There was a notice, neatly executed, to the right of the door. *Officer Commanding*, it said in a dozen languages, including Hebrew and Arabic.

The front door opened into a small, empty anteroom. Simon crossed to another door at the far end and knocked.

A voice ordered them to "Come," and Simon gestured, smartly barking out, "Commander James Bond, sir."

Given everything that he'd seen outside, and with the myriad questions unanswered, Bond would not have been shaken to find Rolling Joe Zwingli on the other side of the door. But the identity of the man seated behind the folding table that dominated the office made him catch his breath with surprise.

There was certainly some connection between this man and Zwingli, for the last time Bond had seen him was in the Salles Privées at Monte Carlo.

"Come in, Commander Bond. Come in. Welcome to Erewhon," said Tamil Rahani, their suspect tycoon. "Do sit down. Get the commander a chair, Simon."

– 11 –

Terror for Hire

THE ROOM, LARGE AND UTILITARIAN, con-
tained the folding table, four chairs, and filing cabinet
that could have been found in the quartermaster's
stores of most armies the world over. The furnishings
also appeared to reflect the character of Tamil
Rahani, the officer commanding.

From a distance, when Bond had viewed him
briefly in Monte Carlo, Rahani had looked like any
other successful businessman—sleek, well-dressed,
needle-sharp and confident. At close quarters, the
confidence certainly remained, but instead of sleek-
ness a kind of dynamism stood out—harnessed and
controlled. One usually got the same sense of self-
discipline from very good military leaders, a kind of

147

quiet calm, through which one detected, rather than viewed, an immense, unflinching resolve, coupled with authority and the subject's own firm belief in his ability. All these things were present, emanating from Tamil Rahani like static electricity.

As Simon brought the chair—and took one for himself—Bond glanced quickly around the office. The walls were lined with maps, charts, large posters displaying the silhouettes of aircraft, ships, tanks and other armored vehicles. There were also year- and month-planners, their red, green and blue markers giving the only splash of color to an otherwise functional ambience.

"Don't I know you, sir?" Bond was careful to observe military courtesy, for Rahani's final detectable attribute was danger.

Rahani laughed, throwing back his head a fraction. "You may have seen pictures in newspapers, Commander. Possibly we shall speak of it later. At the moment I'd rather talk about *you*." His smile puffed out his cheeks, slightly out of character, more like some pompous little chairbound British major. "You come to us highly recommended."

"Really?" It was meant to sound as though Bond could not care a damn whether he came recommended or not.

"Yes," Rahani tapped his teeth with a pencil. The teeth were perfect—white, regular and well-tended, the mustache above them trimmed as if to a regulation length. "Let me be completely frank with you, Commander. Nobody knows whether you can be trusted or not. Everybody—and by that I mean most of the major intelligence communities of the world—knows that you have been a loyal and active officer of the British Secret Intelligence Service for a long time. You ceased to be either a member or active some time ago. It is said that you resigned in a fit of bitterness." He made a small questioning noise, like a hum in the back of his throat. "It is also said that *nobody* ever goes private from the SIS, the CIA, Mossad or the KGB—is that the correct term? Going private?"

"So the espionage writers tell us." Bond maintained his couldn't-care-less attitude.

"Well," Rahani continued, "quite a number of people wanted to find out the truth. A number of agencies would have liked to approach you. One very nearly did. But they got cold feet. It was argued that, having been loyal for so long, you would most probably rediscover your loyalty if put to the test—no matter how disaffected you felt."

There was a pause, during which Bond remained poker-faced until the officer commanding spoke again.

"You're either an exceptional actor, Commander, working under professional instructions, or you are genuine. What appears to be true is that you're a man of uncommon ability in your field; alas, you're out of work. If there is truth in the rumors surrounding your resignation, then it seems a pity to allow you to remain unemployed. The purpose of bringing you here is to test the story, and, possibly, offer you a job. You would like to work? In intelligence, of course?"

"Depends," his voice flat as a board.

"On what?" Sharp, the man of authority showing through.

"On the job." Bond's face relaxed a fraction. "Look, sir. I don't wish to appear rude, but I *was* brought here—wherever it may be—against my will. Also, my previous career is nobody's business but mine—and, I suppose, the people for whom I used to work. To be honest, I'm so fed up with the trade that I'm not at all certain if I really want to get mixed up in it again."

"Not even as an adviser? Not even with a very high salary? With little to do, and less danger in doing it?"

"I just don't know."

"Then would you consider a proposition?"

"I'm always open to propositions."

Rahani took a long breath through his nose. "An income in excess of a quarter of a million pounds, sterling, a year. The occasional trip, at short notice, to advise in one country or another. One week out of every two months spent giving a short series of lectures here."

"Where's here?"

For the first time, Rahani's brow puckered with

displeasure. "In good time, Commander. As I've said, in good time."

"Advise on what? Lecture on what?"

"Lecture on the structure and methods of the British Secret Intelligence Service, and the Security Service. Advise on the intelligence and security aspects of certain operations."

"Operations carried out by whom?"

Rahani spread his hands in a gesture of openness. "That would depend. It would also alter from operation to operation. You see, the organization I command bears no allegiance to any one country, group of people or ideal. We are—a much-used word, but the only one—we are apolitical."

Bond waited, as though asking for more details before he committed himself.

"I am a soldier," Rahani finally gave in. "I have been a mercenary in my time. I am also a highly successful businessman. We have certain things in common, I think. One of them being a liking for money. Some time ago, and in cooperation with one or two other like-minded people, I saw a possibility of combining the two things—mercenary activities and very profitable business returns. Being apolitical myself, owing nothing to political ideologies or beliefs, it was easy. Countries, and groups of so-called revolutionaries, are always in need of specialists. Either a particular man, or a group of men—even a planning group, and the soldiery to carry out the plan."

"Rent-A-Terrorist," Bond said, with a touch of distaste. "Who does not dare hires someone else to dare for him. It's a truly mercenary activity, in all senses of the word."

"Well put. Yes, but you'd be surprised, Commander Bond. The so-called terrorist organizations are not our only customers. Bona fide governments have been known to ask for an operation, with percentage payment on results. Anyway, as a former intelligence officer you cannot allow yourself the luxury of politics, or ideals."

"I can allow myself the luxury of opposing certain ideals. Even of intensely disliking them."

"And, it seems, you have an intense dislike for the British and American way of intelligence—yes?"

"Let's just say I'm disillusioned; that I'm embittered that an official organization can call me to question after many years of loyal service."

"Don't you ever feel that revenge could be sweet?"

"I'd be a liar if I said it hadn't crossed my mind, but it's never been an obsession. I don't harbor grudges."

Rahani made the querying, humming noise again. "We shall need your cooperation; and your decision. You understand what I mean?"

Bond nodded, saying he was no fool. Having disclosed the existence, and purpose, of his organization, Tamil Rahani was committed to making a decision about Bond. If he could offer a job—and if Bond accepted—there was no problem. If, however, he decided Bond was a risk, or his motives were in doubt, there could only be one answer. During this last summary, Bond never once used Rahani's real name. It would not do, at this stage, to disclose the knowledge.

Rahani heard him out. Then—

"You won't mind if I ask a few pertinent questions?"

"What do you call pertinent?"

"I'd like to know the things you would not discuss with the Press. The *true* reason for your resignation, Commander Bond. An interdepartment disagreement, I believe you said. Accusations, which were withdrawn, but taken most seriously by yourself."

"If I don't choose to tell you?"

Rahani's smile was there. "Then we have to conclude that you are not trustworthy, my friend. A conclusion that may have unpleasant consequences."

Bond went through the process of looking as though he was giving the situation some thought. With M and Bill Tanner he had put together a story that would hold water up to a point. To prove, or disprove, this version would mean getting hard information from the Judicial Branch—a number of experienced barristers retained by the Service, also from three definite individuals working in the Registry and someone who had easy access to the documents held by S Department.

After a couple of minutes Bond gave a short nod. "Right. If you want the truth . . ."

"Good. Tell us then, Commander Bond." The voice and manner were equally bland.

He told the story, just as they had concocted it in M's office. Over a period of some six months it had been discovered that several highly sensitive files had been taken from the Service Headquarters and kept out overnight. It was an old story, and one that was technically possible, even with the stringent security, spot checks, and signing in and out of files.

However, the system was double-checked by using an electronic bar code, appended to each file, and read in every time the file was taken out or returned. The files went in—and out—via a machine that read the code and stored the information in the Registry databank, which was examined at the end of each month. It was impossible to alter the bar codes on the files, or to duplicate them. But because the information, stored away on the big computer tapes, was only read out at the end of each month, one person could return a dummy file each night—if he so wished—putting back the original the following night. By alternating dummy and original it was possible to examine at leisure around twenty files over a month before anyone discovered the tampering. This, Bond maintained, had occurred—though Registry had spent so much time cross-checking, and looking at the data, because they imagined it to be a program error in the computer, that a further week had passed before a report went up to Head of Service.

In all, only eight files had been at risk. But, on the relevant dates, James Bond had been one of those with access to the files. Five people were under suspicion, and they had hauled Bond in before anybody else.

"Someone of my rank, experience and service would normally be given the courtesy of a private interview with the Head of Service," he said, his tone verging on rising anger. "But no. It didn't seem to matter that the other four were junior, relatively inexperienced, and without field records. It was as if I was singled out because of my position; because I had been in the field; because of my experience."

"You were actually accused?" It was Simon who asked.

Bond simulated the anger now boiling up and breaking the surface. "Oh, yes. Yes, I was accused. Before they even talked to anyone else they carted in a couple of very good interrogators, and a QC. 'You removed these files from the headquarters building, Commander Bond. Why? Did you copy them? Who asked you to take them?'—It went on for two days."

"And did you take them from the building, Commander?"

"No, I did not," Bond shouted. "And it took them

155

another two days to haul in the other four, and then a day for Head of Registry to come back off leave and recall that special permission had been given to one officer to take the wretched files over for study by a Civil Service mandarin—adviser to the Ministry. They had left spaces in the records, just to keep the data neat. Head of Registry was supposed to put a special code into the databank. But he was off on leave, and forgot about it. Nobody had a go at him, or offered his head on a salver."

"So no files went missing at all. You got an apology, of course?"

"Not immediately," Bond glowered, like a schoolboy. "And nobody seemed the least bit concerned about my feelings. Head of Service didn't appear to even understand why I got annoyed."

"So you resigned? Just like that?"

"More or less."

"It's a very good story," Tamil Rahani looked pleased. "But it is one that will be difficult to prove, if I know anything about government departments."

"Exceptionally difficult," Bond agreed.

"Tell me, what did the questionable files contain?"

"Ah," Bond tried to look as charming as possible. "Now you're really asking me to betray."

"Yes." Matter-of-fact.

"Mainly updated material concerning the disposition of Eastern bloc tactical nuclear weapons. One concerned agents on the ground and their proximity to the Eastern bases."

Rahani's eyebrows twitched. "Sensitive. I see. Well, Commander, you've started, so you might as well finish. I shall make a few tiny inquiries. In the meantime, perhaps Simon will show you around Erewhon, and we'll continue to have our talks."

"You mean interrogations?"

Rahani shrugged. "If you like. Your future, salary and work, depend on what you tell us now. Quite painless, I assure you."

As they reached the door, Bond turned back. "May I ask *you* a question, sir?"

"Of course."

"You bear a striking resemblance to a Mr. Tamil Rahani—chairman of Rahani Electronics. I believe you've been in Monte Carlo recently?"

Rahani's laugh had all the genuine warmth of an angry cobra. "You should know, Commander. You were raising a fair amount of hell at the gaming tables on the Cote d'Azur at the time, I think."

"Touché, sir." He followed Simon out into the sunshine.

They went first to a mess hall where around eighty people were enjoying a lunch of chicken, seasoned and cooked with peppers, onions, almonds and garlic.

Everyone wore the same olive-drab uniform, and some carried sidearms. There were men and women, mainly young and from many different countries. They sat in pairs, or teams of four. That was how the training went, Simon explained. They worked with a partner, or in teams. Sometimes two teams would be put together, if the work demanded it. Also, some of the pairs were training to be lone specialists.

"In what?"

"Oh, we cover the usual spectrum. Big bang merchants; take-away artists; removal men; monopoly teams. You name it, we do it—electricians, mechanics, drivers, all the necessary humdrum jobs also."

Bond translated the jargon as meaning explosives experts; kidnappers, or thieves; assassins; and hijack or hostage teams. He identified a number of different tongues being spoken—there were Germans, French, Italians, Arabs, Israelis, Irish, and even English. He almost immediately identified a pair of German terrorists whose names and details were on file with his Service, MI5 and Scotland Yard.

"If you want anonymity, I shouldn't use those two in Europe," he told Simon, quietly. "They've both got star billing with our people."

"That's good. Thank you. We prefer unknowns, and I had a feeling about that couple. Everyone has had some field work behind them when they come here—how else would they lose their ideals?—but we do not like 'faces.'" He gave a pleasant grin. "But we have need of them. Some have to be lost, you know. It comes in handy during training."

Throughout the afternoon, they walked around the training area, which was incredibly well-equipped, and Bond experienced the odd sensation of having seen all this before—taking part in it, but as though through a different end of a telescope.

It took an hour or so to work out exactly what was wrong. These men and women were being trained in techniques he had seen used by the SAS, Germany's GSG9, the French GIGN, and several other elite police, military and paramilitary units that deal with antiterrorist activities. There was one difference, however. The trainees at Erewhon were receiving expert tuition on how to counter antiterrorist action.

Apart from classes in weaponry of all kinds, explosives and the like, there was very special training on hijacking and takeover, leaving little to chance. They even had two real flight simulators within the compound, while one building was devoted solely to the techniques of bargaining with authorities while holding either hostages or kidnap victims.

One of the most spectacular training aids lay around the gutted buildings Bond had earlier noticed. Here a team of four would be taught how to counter attempted rescues by men using all the known techniques of well-trained counterterrorist forces. It was disturbing to note that most eventualities appeared to be covered.

That night he slept again in the same unfurnished, secure building in which he had woken; and, on the following day, the hours of interrogation began.

It was done on a classic one-to-one basis—Tamil Rahani and James Bond—with Rahani ingeniously asking seemingly ordinary questions that, when expanded and probed, turned out to be attempts to pry loose highly sensitive information concerning Bond's Service.

They began with reasonably harmless stuff—organization and channels of command; but soon, the detail was being called for, and Bond had to use all his native ingenuity to give the appearance of telling everything, while keeping back truly vital information.

But Rahani was like a terrier. Just when Bond thought he had managed to retain some real piece of information, the officer commanding Erewhon would change tack, going in a circle to return to the nub of the question. Soon, it became all too obvious that, once they had milked him dry, Bond would be quietly thrown to the wolves.

It happened on the sixth day. Rahani had been hammering away at the same questions—which concerned minutiae of protection for heads of state, the Prime Minister, the Queen and other members of the Royal Family. This, naturally, was no part of Bond's own work, nor the work of his Service, but Rahani, quite rightly, assumed that he would have a great deal of knowledge about the subject.

160

He even wanted names, possible weaknesses in those assigned to such duties, and the kind of schedules they worked.

At about five o'clock in the afternoon, a message was brought in. Rahani read it, then slowly folded the paper neatly, and looked at Bond.

"Well, Commander, it seems your days here are numbered. There is a job for you back in England. Something very important is at last coming to fruition, and you are to be part of it. You are on salary as of now." He picked up one of his two telephones, asking for Simon to come over as quickly as possible. They all used simple first names at Erewhon, with the exception of the officer commanding.

"Commander Bond is with us," he told Simon. "There's work for him, and he leaves for England tomorrow. You will escort him." An odd look passed between the two men before Rahani continued. "But, Simon, we have yet to see the gallant commander in action. Would it be a good idea to put him through the Charnel House?"

"He'd like that, I'm sure, sir." The Charnel House was a gallows-humor nickname for the gutted buildings they used for training in defense against a counterterrorist force.

Simon said he would set things up, and they all left for the short walk over to the area where Simon left to make the arrangements. "I've got just the team for you, James." He gave a knowing look, which

Bond felt had some hidden meaning that he should be able to decipher. Ten minutes later, Simon returned, taking Bond inside the house.

Though the place was gutted and bore the marks of many simulated battles, it had been remarkably well built. A large entrance hall stood inside the solid main door. Two short passages led off to left and right, ending in doors that opened onto large rooms. The rooms were uncarpeted but contained one or two pieces of furniture. A solid staircase climbed from the hall to a wide landing. The wall was blank except for one door, through which one reached a long passage running the length of the house's rear. Doors on the front-facing wall led into two rooms built directly above the ones on the ground floor.

Simon led him upstairs. "They have a team of four. Blank ammunition, of course, but real 'flash-bangs,'"—flash-bangs were stun grenades, not the nicest thing to be near on detonation. "The brief is that they know you are somewhere upstairs," he pulled out the ASP 9mm. "Nice weapon, James. Very nice. Who would think it has the power of a .44 Magnum?"

"You've been playing with my toys."

"Thoroughly. There, one magazine of blanks, and one spare. Use initiative, James. Good luck." Simon looked at his watch. "You have three minutes."

Bond quickly reconnoitered the building and placed himself in the upper corridor, knowing it had no windows. He remained close to the door that opened onto the landing, but well shielded by the corridor wall. He was crouched against the wall when the stun grenades exploded in the hallway below— two ear-splitting crumps, followed by several withering bursts of automatic fire. Bullets hacked and chipped into the plaster and brickwork on the other side of the wall, while another burst almost took the door beside him off its hinges.

They were not using blanks. This was for real, and he knew with sudden shock that it was as he had earlier deduced. He was being thrown to the wolves.

– 12 –

Return to Sender

TWO MORE EXPLOSIONS came from below, followed by another heavy burst of fire. The second team of two men was clearing the ground floor. Bond could hear the feet of the first team on the stairs. In a few seconds there would be the dance of death from the landing—a couple of stun grenades, or smoke canisters, through the door to his right, then lead would hose down the passage, taking him on that short trip into eternity.

Simon's voice kept running in his head like a looped tape—"Use your initiative . . . Use your initiative . . ." Was that a hint? A clue?

Move. Bond was off down the corridor, making for the room to his left. He had some vague idea that he could leap from the window—anything to remove his vulnerable body from the immediate vicinity of the vicious, inevitable hailstorm of bullets.

He took rapid strides, hand closing on the doorknob. He turned it, trying to make as little noise as possible, closed the door behind him and slid a small bolt above the lock, in which there was no key. He started to cross the floor, heading for the windows, clutching the useless ASP as though his life depended on it. Halfway, as he sidestepped a chair, he saw them—two ASP magazines, cutaway matt black oblongs, lying on a rickety table between the high windows. Grabbing at the first, he saw immediately that they were his own reserves, both full, loaded with Glasers.

There is a fast routine for reloading the ASP—a fluid movement that quickly jettisons an empty magazine, replacing it with a full one. Bond went through the reload in a matter of five seconds, including the action of dropping his eyes to check that a live round had entered the chamber.

He performed the whole maneuver on the move, turning his body so that he was hard against the wall to the left of the door. The team would leap in after the grenades had accomplished their disorientating effect—one left and one right. They would be firing as they came, but Bond gambled on their first bursts going wide across the room. As he reloaded, he was conscious of them running down the corridor, then the bangs and rattle of their textbook assault through the door.

Flattening himself against the wall, he held the powerful little weapon at arm's length—the two-handed grip.

Bullets splintered the woodwork to his right. A boot smashed in the handle and lock, while a pair of stun grenades hit the bare boards with a heavy clunk, one of them rolling for a split second before detonation.

He closed his eyes, head turning slightly to avoid the most distressing effect of the little metal eggs—the flash that temporarily blinds—though nothing could stop the great crump that seemed to explode from within his own cranium, putting his head in a vise and ringing in his ears like a magnified bell. His head was crammed with noise and a great buzzing. It blotted all external sounds, even the noise of his own pistol as he fired, and the death-rattle of the sub-machine guns from the two-man team as they stepped through the lingering smoke.

At the first movement through the door, Bond sighted—the three little yellow triangles on the Guttersnipe all falling equally onto the dark moving shape. He squeezed the trigger twice, resighted and squeezed again. In all the four bullets were off in less than three seconds—though the whole scene appeared to be frozen in time, slowed like a cinematic trick so that everything happened with a ponderous, even clumsy, brutality.

The man nearest Bond leaped to his left, the wicked little automatic weapon tucked between upper arm and rib cage, the muzzle already spitting fire as he identified and turned toward his target. Bond's first bullet caught him in the neck, hurling the man sideways, pushing him, his head lolling as though it had been ripped from its body. The second slug entered his head, which literally exploded into a cloud of fine pink and gray.

The third and fourth bullets both caught the second man in the chest, a couple of inches below the windpipe. He was swinging outward and to his right, realizing, too late, where the target was situated, the gun in his hand spraying bullets toward the window.

The ASP's impact lifted the man from his feet, knocking him back so that he was momentarily poised in midair, angled at forty-five degrees from the floor, the machine pistol still firing and ripping into the ceiling as a mushroom of blood sprouted from his torn body.

Because of his temporary deafness, Bond felt as though he stood outside time and action, but experience pushed him on. Two down, he thought, two to go, for the second team would—almost certainly—be covering the entrance hall, might even be coming to their comrades' assistance.

Bond stepped over the headless corpse of the first

intruder, his foot almost slipping in a lake of blood. It always stunned him how there was so much blood from one man. This was something they did not show in movies, or even newsreel film—the gallon, and then some, of blood that fountained from a human body that has been violently cut to pieces by a pair of well-placed shots.

In the doorway, he paused for a second, ears straining to no effect.

Glancing down, he saw that the number two of the team still had a pair of grenades tucked firmly into his belt, hooked on by the safety levers. He slid one out, removed the pin, holding the oval egg in his left hand, and advanced back down the corridor toward the landing door, calculating the amount of force he would need to hurl the object down the stairs. It had to be done right, for he would not get a second chance.

He paused, just short of the landing door, and something made him turn—that sixth sense which, over the years, had been fine-tuned to emergencies. He spun around, just in time to see the figure emerging gingerly, negotiating his way through the gore and shattered bodies on the far side of the door.

Later, Bond reasoned, they had planned some kind of pincer maneuver, one man scaling the wall to attack through the window while his comrades stormed through the interior. He aimed two shots at the man in the doorway, while his left hand lobbed the stun grenade out of the landing door in the direction of the staircase.

He saw the man in the doorway spin as though caught by a violent whirlwind and, at the same instant, felt the flash from the landing.

Five seconds to release the magazine, in which there were now only two rounds left, and replace it with the fully charged one. Then two paces through the door, firing as he went—two slugs going nowhere while he located his target.

The last man was struggling at the bottom of the stairs, for the grenade had caught him napping. From the scorch marks and his agonized flapping at the smoldering cloth around his loins it was obvious that the grenade, which rarely kills, had hit him squarely in the groin.

Still deaf, Bond saw the man's mouth opening and closing, his face distorted. From the top of the stairs, he shot him once—neatly blowing off the top of his head so that he fell onto his back, then bounced a foot or so on impact.

Quietly, Bond retraced his footsteps, once more stepping over the bodies and crossing to the window. Below, and about twenty yards away, Tamil Rahani stood, watching, with Simon and half a dozen members of Erewhon's permanent staff. They were quite still, heads held as though listening. There was no sign of an unholstered weapon, and Bond could not see any other guns trained on the house—from roof-tops or other vantage points.

He moved back from the window, not wanting to show himself yet uncertain of the best, and safest, way to get out of the place. He had gone only two steps, when the decision was partially made for him.

"Are you still with us, Commander Bond?" Rahani's voice drifted up from the warm air outside, followed by Simon's calling, "James? Did you figure it out?"

He returned to the window, standing to one side, showing as little of his head as possible. They were all in the same place as before. Still no visible armament.

Withdrawing, Bond shouted, "You tried to kill me, you bastards. Let's make it fair. I'll take on one of you at a time." He dropped to the ground and snake-crawled along the wall below the window to the next aperture.

They were all looking at the first window as he fired, putting the bullet about ten yards in front of them, kicking up a great cloud of dust.

"Right, Bond." It was Tamil Rahani calling. "No-body wanted to do you any harm. A test, that's all. A test of your efficiency. Just come out now. The test is complete."

"One of you—unarmed. Just one—Simon, if you like. In now. At the front. Otherwise I start taking you out, very quickly." A quick peek. Their reaction was very fast, for Simon was already unbuckling his belt, letting it fall to the ground as he walked forward.

Seconds later, Bond was at the top of the stairs, and Simon stood in the entrance hall, hands on his head, staring with some admiration.

"What's going on exactly?" Bond asked, and Simon looked up.

"Nothing. You did as we expected. Everyone told us how good you were, so we sent in four quite expendable men—two of them were the ones you pointed out to me the other day—the German fellows who you said were known faces. We have others like them. This is a standard exercise."

"Standard? Telling the victim everyone's only using blank ammunition . . . ?"

"Well, you soon discovered you had live rounds, like the others. They also thought they had blanks."

"But I only had live ammunition if I could find it—which I did, partly by luck."

"Rubbish. You had the real thing from the word go, and there were spare magazines all over the place, James. Can I come up?"

Keeping his hands on his head, Simon slowly mounted the stairs, while Bond began to wonder. Fool, he said to himself. You merely took the man's word for it. He said you had blanks, but . . .

Five minutes later, Simon had proved his point—first by retrieving Bond's original magazine, which proved to be fully, and correctly, loaded with Glasers;

second, by showing him other full magazines—on the corridor floor and in the second room upstairs, as well as on the landing.

Even with this evidence, it had still been a fool-hardy and exceptionally dangerous business. Four men armed with, as it turned out, MP 5K submachine guns, against one.

"I could have been wiped out within seconds."

"But you weren't, were you, James? Our information was that you would get out alive, if set this kind of challenge. It merely shows that our informants were correct."

They walked down the stairs and out into the air, which felt very good. Bond had a feeling that he was, indeed, lucky to be alive. He also wondered if his luck was merely a stay of execution.

"And if I had died in there?"

Rahani did not smile at the question. "Then, Commander Bond, we would've only had one body to bury instead of four. You lived; you showed us your reputation is well deserved. Here only survival matters."

"And it was, as Simon said, a challenge? A test?"

"More of a test."

They had dined alone, the three of them. Now they sat in Tamil Rahani's office.

"Please." The officer commanding Erewhon made

an open gesture with his hands. "Please believe me, I would not have put you through this ordeal, had it been up to me."

"It's your organization. You were offering me a job."

Rahani did not look him in the eyes. "Well," he said, his voice low. "I have to be perfectly truthful with you. Yes, the idea of founding an organization that rented out mercenary terrorists *was* my original idea. Unhappily, as so often happens in matters like this, I needed specialist assistance. In turn this meant taking in partners. The end product gives me a large return, but . . . well, I take my orders from others."

"And in this case your orders were . . . ?"

"To make a decision regarding the possibility of using you. To see if you were trustworthy, or merely some kind of undercover plant. To obtain certain information from you, the strength of which we could easily test, and then—when we were satisfied on those points—to put you up against a real challenge: to see if you could survive a genuine situation of danger."

"And I've passed on all points?"

"Correct. We are satisfied. Now, you can be returned to our planners. It was true when I said there was a job waiting for you. There has been from the word go. That is why you were manipulated—and why you were brought here, where we have facilities. You see, once here, if you had turned out to be—how do you people say it?—A double? Is that correct?"

174

Bond nodded.

"If you had been exposed as a double, we had the facilities here for losing you. Permanently."

"So what's this job you have for me?"

"It is a large and complex operation, with many tiny details. But one thing I *can* tell you." He looked up at Bond, his eyes blank as though each was made of glass. "What is being planned at the moment will be the so-called terrorist coup of the decade, even the century. If things proceed normally, they will spark off the ultimate revolution. A unique and complete change in the course of world events, the beginning of a new age. And those of us taking part in it will inherit a large and privileged position within the Phoenix that will undoubtedly spring from what is to be done."

"I saw the film."

Simon rose, going over to the filing cabinet on which rested a few bottles. He poured himself a liberal glass of wine, then disappeared from Bond's view.

"Scoff, Mr. Bond. But I think even you will find this to be an operation without parallel in history."

"And it won't work without me?" Bond raised a cynical eyebrow.

"I did not say that. But it may not work without somebody *like* you, Commander Bond."

"Okay." He leaned back in his chair. "So tell me all about it."

"I'm afraid *I* can't do that." The cold eyes bored into him, so that, for a second or two, Bond thought the man was trying out some elementary hypnosis.

"So?"

"So, you have to be returned. You have to go back."

"Back? Back to where?"

Too late Bond felt Simon's presence behind him.

"Back from whence you came, James."

Bond was conscious of the small, sharp pinch through his shirt, on his arm just below the right shoulder.

Tamil Rahani continued to speak.

"We're not talking about the stories dreamed up by pulp novelists. No blackmail through concealed nuclear devices hidden in the heart of great Western cities; no plots to kidnap the President, or hold the world to ransom by setting all the major currencies at naught. We're not talking about extortion; nor . . . are . . . we . . ." His voice slowly receded, fogged over, and then—like life itself—went out.

– 13 –

The Numbers Racket

THE SKY WAS GRAY, almost leaden. He could see it through the window—the sky and part of an old apple tree. That was all.

Bond had woken from what seemed to be natural sleep. He was still fully dressed, and the ASP, complete with holster and one extra clip of ammunition, lay on the bedside table. The room appeared to be very English—white gloss paint on the woodwork and Laura Ashley wallpaper, with contrasting fabrics for curtains. Only most of the window was bricked up; and the door would not budge when he tried to open it.

There was a depressing sense of déjà vu. He had been along this road before, only last time it was

Erewhon. Rahani had said they had accepted him, but he wondered how and why. Certainly the long interrogation sessions had been searching, and M had instructed him to give away anything they could check on, even if it was highly sensitive. Fences, his Chief maintained, could be mended later. But what would be the state of play by the time they came to mend fences? At Erewhon preparations were steaming forward for something earth-shattering. What was it that Rahani had said?—"A unique and complete change in the course of world events." The dream of revolutionaries—to change the march of history; to crush the status quo; to alter in order to build a new society. Well, Bond thought, it had been done before, but only within countries. Russia was the prime example, though Hitler's rise in Germany had been a revolution as well. The problem with revolutions, so history taught, was that the ideal usually fell short because of human frailty.

Also, Rahani had specifically told him that he—Bond—or somebody like him, was essential to whatever was about to take place. They needed a man, or woman, with the skills or contacts or knowledge of an experienced Secret Intelligence field officer. What part of those skills, or what particular piece of knowledge was required?

He was still pondering on these things when somebody knocked at the door, and a key turned in the lock.

Cindy Chalmer looked bright and crisp. She wore a laboratory coat over jeans and shirt, and was carrying a large tray. "Breakfast, Mr. Bond," she beamed at him. In the background, he glimpsed a tall, muscular man—a hood if ever he had seen one.

Bond nodded toward him. "Someone to watch over me?"

"And me, I guess." She set the tray down on the end of the bed. "Can't be too careful with hot shots like you around. Nobody knew what you'd like, so Dazzle did the full English breakfast—bacon, eggs, sausages, toast, coffee." She lifted the silver cover from the steaming plate, holding it with the inside toward Bond. There was a folded paper neatly taped to the inside of the cover.

"That'll do fine." He gave her an understanding nod. "Do I call room service when I've finished?"

"Don't call us, we'll call you," she said brightly. "We will, Mr. Bond. I gather the Professor wants to talk with you later. Good to see you feeling better. They said you had a nasty bump when you went off the road. The Professor was genuinely worried, that's why he persuaded the hospital to let him bring you here."

"Very good of him."

She seemed to linger by the door. "Well, it's nice to know we'll all be working together."

"Good to have a job in these difficult times," Bond countered, not knowing how much Cindy knew. Had they told her he'd been in a motor accident? That he was being given a job at Endor? Well, presumably the latter was more or less true. He waited until the key clunked home in the lock. There was nothing else to hear, no retreating footsteps, for the passage outside—like this room—was overlaid with thick carpet.

The paper came away easily from the inside of the lid. Cindy had filled it with small, neat writing and, in spite of the steam, the ink had not run. The note started abruptly, without any salutation.

> I don't know what's happened. They say you've had a car smash, but I don't know whether to believe them. The facts are simple. They brought your Bentley back here, and there's been a lot of talk about you joining the team as a programer. I wondered if they knew you had computer equipment with you, and felt you would not want them to find it. Very difficult, but I got hold of the Bentley's keys and cleaned out the boot. All your private stuff is now hidden in the garage, and not likely to be found, unless we're unlucky. A good thing I did it straight away, because security's been tightened for the weekend. A lot of people are coming down, and—from what I've heard—the game I spoke of (remember the balloons?) is going to be in use. It is possible that I may be

180

able to get hold of it. Do you wish to copy?
Or is that superfluous now that you are
"One of Us?" C.

So, the place was going to be crowded, The Balloon Game was to the fore, and Bond, so he'd been told, was essential. Therefore, if The Balloon Game was a training simulation for the operation, then Bond and the game were closely interconnected. QED.

He tore the message into tiny pieces and ate them with the bacon and some toast. He could not stomach the eggs or sausage, but the coffee was good, and he drank four cups, strong and black.

There was a small bathroom attached to his bedroom and set neatly on the glass shelf, above the handbasin, were his toilet articles—everything from razor to his favorite cologne. Already he had seen his weekend case beside the small wardrobe, and on examination discovered his clothes had all been washed and neatly pressed.

Don't believe it all, he told himself. On the face of it, he was trusted—weapon, shaving kit, everything intact. But they kept the door locked, and there was no immediate way out of the window.

He showered, shaved and changed, retaining the casual clothes that allowed him to move easily and fast. Even the ASP was strapped to his right hip by the time a second knock and the turning of the key announced the arrival of two muscular men whose faces were definitely familiar from the files—"Tigerbalm" Balmer and "Happy" Hopcraft.

"Mornin', Mr. Bond." Tigerbalm smiled, his eyes not meeting Bond's but sliding around the room, as though measuring it.

"Hallo, James, nice ter meecher." Happy stuck out a hand, but Bond pretended not to notice.

"Balmer and Hopcraft," Tigerbalm said. "At your service. The Professor wants a word." Behind the expensive mohair suits and the cheerful bonhomie lay a sinister spark of menace. One knew, just by looking at them, that this pair would have your head, stuffed and mounted, if it suited them, or if they were so ordered by someone paying them for the favor.

"Well, if the Professor calls, we must answer." Bond looked at the key, clutched in Tigerbalm's hand. "That really necessary?"

"Orders." From Happy.

"Let's go and see the Professor, then."

They did not exactly crowd him as the three of them went down the corridor, then the stairs, and on to the working area that had once been the cellars, but their presence had a certain intimidating effect. Bond felt that one false move—any inclination to go in another direction—would bring about a fast, restraining action.

There was no sign of either Cindy or Peter, but St. John-Finnes sat at his desk, the large computer console in front of him, and the VDU giving out a glow of color.

"James, it's nice to have you back." He signaled with his head, indicating that Tigerbalm and Happy should leave, then gestured to an easy chair.

"Well," when they were settled, "I'm sorry you were put to some inconvenience."

"I could've been killed, quite easily." Bond spoke in a level, calm manner.

"Yes. Yes, I'm sorry about that; but it was actually *you* who did the killing, I gather."

"Only because I had to. Habits take a long time to die. I think my reactions are reasonably fast."

The high, birdlike head moved up and down in comprehension. "Yes, the reports all say you're rather good. You must understand that we had to be sure of you. I mean, one error and a great deal of money, and planning, would have been in jeopardy."

Bond said nothing, so St. John-Finnes continued: "Anyway, you passed with flying colors. I'm glad, because we need you. You're now aware of the connection between things here at Endor and the training camp, Erewhon?"

"I gather that you and your partner, Mr. Tamil Rahani, run a rather strange enterprise—hiring out mercenaries to terrorist and revolutionary groups."

"Oh, a little more than that." It was the benign large bird, smiling and nodding. "We can offer complete packages. A group can come to us with an idea, and we do everything else—from raising the money to performing the operation. For instance, the job for which you have been recruited has been on the drawing board for some time now, and we stand to gain a great deal from it."

Bond said he realized that he had been vetted, tested; also he knew there was some particular job for him, within the organization, and connected to an operation. "But I've no idea of the . . ."

"Details? No, of course you have no idea. Just as in your old profession people worked on a need-to-know basis, so we must be exceptionally careful—particularly with this current work. No one person is in possession of the full picture, with the exception of Colonel Rahani and myself, of course." He made a slight movement of the fingers and head, which was meant to convey modesty. It was a curiously Oriental gesture, as though he wished Bond to realize that he was really unworthy to be granted the honor of knowing such plans. Bond also noted that it was now *Colonel* Rahani, and he wondered where that title came from.

". . . particularly careful concerning you, I fear," St. John-Finnes had spoken again. "Our principals were very much against giving you a situation of trust, but I think—since Erewhon—we have made them think twice."

"This job? The one you've recruited me for . . . ?" Bond started.

184

"Has been in the making for a considerable time. Much money was needed, and our principals in the matter were, shall we say, short of funds. This suited us. We're packagers, Bond. So we packaged some money-making projects to finance the main thrust."

"Hence the Kruxator Collection, and other pieces of high-tech thieving."

Jay Autem Holy remained blizzard cold. Only in his eyes could Bond detect a tiny wariness. "You come to interesting deductions, my dear Bond. For one who knows nothing . . ."

"Stab in the dark." Bond's face betrayed nothing. "After all, there have been several imaginative robberies lately—all with the same handwriting. A case of putting two and two together, and, maybe, coming in with the correct answer."

Holy made a noncommittal grunt. "Good. I am satisfied that you're clean, Bond. But my orders are to segregate you. There is knowledge, and skill, which you possess. We require you to put that knowledge into action now."

"Well?"

"Well, as a former field officer of the Secret Intelligence Service, you must have a working knowledge of the diplomatic, and military, communications network."

"Yes."

"Tell me, then, do you know what an EPOC Frequency is?"

"Yes." Bland as before, though Bond was now beginning to worry. The last time he had heard of EPOC Frequencies was when he had been called upon to guard against possible aggressive monitoring of signals during a visit to Europe by the President of the United States. EPOC stood for Emergency Presidential Orders Communications. So an EPOC Frequency was the cleared radio band frequency upon which flash—or emergency—messages were sent out by the United States President during an official tour outside the United States.

"And what kind of signal is sent over an EPOC Frequency?"

Bond paused, as though giving the matter some thought. "Only vital military instructions. Sometimes a response to a military query that demands action from the President only. Sometimes action inaugurated by him."

"And how are these orders transmitted?"

"Usual high-speed traffic, but on a line kept permanently clear, via one of the communications satellites."

"No, I mean the nature of the transmissions. The form they take."

"Oh. A simple group of digits. Data, I suppose. The orders that can be given through the EPOC Frequency are very limited. It's rarely used, you know."

"Quite." Holy gave what could only be described

186

as a knowing smile. "Rarely used, and very limited—but limited in a most far-reaching way, yes?"

Bond agreed. "The President would use the EPOC Frequency only on strong recommendation from his military advisers. The subjects are usually concerned with rapid deployment of conventional troops and weapons . . ."

"The raising, or lowering, of any readiness state as far as nuclear strike capacity is concerned?"

"That's a priority, yes."

"And tell me, would the instructions be obeyed? Immediately, I mean? Suppose the President was, for the sake of argument, in Venice and wished to bring NATO forces to a top level of readiness and prepare his nuclear strike forces for imminent action. Would it simply be done? Without consultation?"

"Quite possibly. The code for that kind of action is, in effect, a computer program. Once it's fed into the system it works. In the scenario you're suggesting, the British Prime Minister and the Commander-in-Chief NATO would consult back. But the readiness state would persist."

"And if the British Prime Minister, and the C-in-C NATO forces, were known to be with the President at the moment of transmission?"

Suddenly they were on very dangerous ground. Bond felt his stomach turn over. Then he remem-

187

bered Rahani's words: *No blackmail . . . no plots to kidnap the President, or hold the world to ransom . . .*

"In those circumstances," he said calmly, thinking meanwhile that something far more devious, more ingenious, than a harebrained revolutionary plot was involved, "the instructions would go to all local commanders automatically. They would be fed into the mainframe computers, the program would begin to run, globally, straight away. No question. But surely you know all of this yourselves."

"Indeed I do." There was a weird, unsettling tranquility in the way Jay Autem answered. "Yourselves" became "I," Bond noticed, and the tone was of an almost glacial imperturbability. "Yes, *I* know the minutiae of it. Just as I know who has access to the daily ciphers for use through the EPOC Frequency; and who also has access to that Frequency."

"Tell me?" Bond gave the impression of not knowing such details.

"Come, Mr. Bond. You know as well as I do."

"I'd rather hear it from you, sir."

"There are only eleven ciphers that are capable of being sent via EPOC. These are seldom altered, for, as you say, they are programs designed to automatically be set in motion while the President is out of the country. The eleventh is, incidentally, a countermand program to stop an order, returning things to the status quo. But that one can be used in only a limited time scale. The Frequency itself is altered at midnight every two days. Correct?"

"I believe so."

"The ciphers are carried by that omnipresent, and somewhat frightening official known as the Bag Man. Correct?"

"The system has been found reliable," Bond observed. "There was a Bag Man present in JFK's entourage in Dallas. It's never been changed. He's always around—in the United States as well as when the Chief Executive travels abroad. The penalty for having your President as C-in-C Armed Forces."

"The Bag Man can only part with the ciphers and EPOC Frequency to the President, or the Vice-President, should anything happen. If the President should meet with a fatal accident overseas, the ciphers are immediately null and void, unless the Vice-President is with him."

"Yes."

"So, if someone—anyone—was in possession of the EPOC Frequency, and the eleven ciphers, it would be possible to relay a particular command that would automatically begin to run?"

For the first time since they had started talking, Bond smiled, slowly shaking his head. "No. There is a failsafe. The EPOC Frequency is a beamed satellite signal. It goes directly through one of the Defense Communications Satellite Systems, and they are very

189

tricky little beggars. When the signal is initiated, the program will only run if the satellite confirms that it has come directly from the area in which it knows—because it has been told—the President is located. You'd have to be *very* close to the President of the United States before you could beat the system and plunge the world into chaos."

"Exactly." To Bond's surprise, Jay Autem Holy looked quite happy. "Would you be surprised to learn that we already have the eleven ciphers, the programs?"

"Nothing surprises me anymore. If you're playing games with an Emergency Presidential Order you still have to get hold of the Frequency for the particular forty-eight hours in which you plan to operate. Then you have to get close to the President, and have means of using the Frequency. I'd say the last two were the hardest—getting near to the President with the equipment needed to transmit, and obtaining the necessary frequency."

"So who else knows the EPOC Frequency—always?" Jay Autem raised his eagle brows, questioning. "I'll tell you, Mr. Bond. The duty Intelligence officer at the NATO C-in-C's headquarters; the duty Communications officer at the CIA HQ, Langley; the duty Communications officer, NSA; the senior communications officers in the United States Armed Forces; and, Mr. Bond, the senior monitoring officer at GCHQ, Cheltenham; plus the Duty Security Officer at the British Foreign Office—who is always a member of the Secret Intelligence Service. It's quite a list, when you consider that the President himself has no knowledge of the EPOC Frequency until he has occasion to use it."

"They're so very rarely used. Yes, as I remember it, you've got the list right—but for one other person."

"Who?"

"The officer who controls the ciphers and frequency at the outset. Usually a communications security officer with the NSA—the National Security Agency."

"Who usually, Mr. Bond, has forgotten the details within five minutes. What we shall need from you is the precise EPOC Frequency on a particular day—which means we need it twenty-four hours in advance. All other details are taken care of."

"And how do you expect me to give you the EPOC Frequency?"

Jay Autem Holy gave a throaty laugh. "You have done service as Duty Security Officer at the Foreign Office. You know the system, and the routine. We know you can be ruthless, and that you are a professional. Someone of your background, with your expertise and knowledge, should have no difficulty in obtaining what we require. Using your knowledge, and what contacts are left to you, there should be no problem. Just put your mind to it. Then report your scheme to me. This is why you were the obvious candidate, Bond. Providing you're as straight as we believe. There is an old proverb—When you want something from the lions, send a lion, not a man."

"I've never heard that before."

"No? You are the lion going to the lions. You are trusted, but if you should fail us . . . Well, we are not forgiving people, I'm afraid. Incidentally, I'm not surprised you didn't recognize the proverb. I just invented it!" And the man who was Jay Autem Holy threw back his head in a guffaw of laughter.

James Bond did not think it was that funny.

"You'll get the Frequency for us, won't you, Bond?" The query came out through a series of deep breaths, as Holy gained control of himself. "Think of it as your revenge. I promise you it will be used for good, and not to create havoc and disaster."

There was no other option, for the moment. "Yes, yes, of course I'll do it. It's only a few numbers you want, after all."

"That's right. You're in the numbers racket now. A few simple digits, James Bond." He paused, the amazing green eyes boring into Bond's skull. "Did you know the Soviets use almost an identical method when the General Secretary and Chairman of the Central Committee is abroad? They call it the Panic Frequency—but in Russian of course."

"You need access to this Panic Frequency as well?" Casual, but with antennae twitching.

"Oh, we *have* access. You're not the only person in the numbers racket, Bond. Our principals in this operation have little money to spare, but they certainly have contacts. Light on cash but heavy on information."

"Ah, your principals, yes." Bond turned down the corners of his mouth. "Even though my part in all this is vital—essential—I am not allowed to know . . . ?"

"The name of our principals? I should have thought a man like you would have already guessed. A once powerful and very rich organization, which has fallen on bad times—mainly because they have lost their last two leaders under tragic circumstances. Our principals, Mr. Bond, are a group who call themselves SPECTRE. The Special Executive for Counterintelligence, Terrorism, Revenge and Extortion. I rather like the Revenge element, don't you?"

– 14 –
Bunker Hill

TIGERBALM AND HAPPY, the strong-arm men in residence, cheerfully took Bond back to his room and left him. Yet there was something different on the return trip. He knew it, but for the moment, preoccupied, could not work out what it was.

Stretching out on the bed, Bond stared at the ceiling and concentrated on the current problem. It all seemed so unreal, particularly in this pleasant room, with its white gloss paint, straight out of a television ad, and the chintzlike pattern of the wallpaper. Yet here he was, with the full knowledge that somewhere below him a scientist who had already run simulations for criminal activities, was now training people for some other, more dangerous mission, this time in the

service of Bond's old, long-standing enemy, SPEC-
TRE.

It didn't surprise him in the least to have learned
that SPECTRE—as principals in the matter—had not
approved of Bond's recruitment. After all, their
death feud had gone on for more years than either
party cared to remember.

But that was neither here nor there at this moment. Jay Autem Holy had disclosed the reason for
Bond's being on the payroll: They needed him. Now,
it was up to him to be convincing, to Holy, Rahani
and SPECTRE, in the role they had designed for
him.

M had been clear on this point. "If they take you
in—if any organization takes you in—then you will
have to split yourself in two," M had ordered. First,
Bond should not believe any recruitment was either
serious or long-term; second, he *had* to believe it was
serious. "If they want you for a specialist job, then
you must, at all costs, treat it as a reality. Work it out,
as they would expect you to: like a professional."

So now, lying on the bed, with part of his mind
reviewing the situation with grave suspicion, James
Bond began to tackle the problem of how to get hold
of the EPOC Frequency.

First, there was a small ray of hope. To secure the
set of numbers they required, he would have to get in
touch with the outside. More, it would mean com-
munication with his old professional world. It was

also ninety-nine percent certain that this contact would, at some point, have to be physical—which meant escape. In this context, M's paradox became crystal clear. He really *had* to set up a method of laying hands on the EPOC Frequency. At the same time, a way had to be devised for him to do it with full knowledge of his own Service.

It took half an hour for Bond to develop two possible methods, though both presupposed a situation in which he alone would be let loose to gain access to the Frequency. The first plan also needed Cindy Chalmer's assistance, and a method of reaching his Bentley. If this was not possible, then the second plan would have to suffice, though it contained a number of imponderables, some of which could come unbuttoned with worrisome ease.

He was still mentally wrestling with this reserve plan when he suddenly realized what was different. Once Tigerbalm and Happy left, there had been no click of key in lock.

Sliding quietly off the bed he went over to the door. It opened without resistance. An error? Or a message from the master of Endor, telling him he was free to go wherever he liked? If the latter, then Bond would have put money on it being a very limited rein. Then why not put it to the test?

The corridor took him out to a landing, the landing to the main staircase, which brought him into the hall, familiar from his previous visit. There, all possibility of real freedom ended. Seated near the door, dressed in jeans and a rollneck, was a young man he recognized from Erewhon. Another graduate from that particular alma mater lounged near the door to the cellar, or laboratory, stairs.

Giving each guard a friendly nod of recognition—returned with only a hint of uncertainty in the far reaches of their eyes—he strolled through to the main drawing room, in which he had last sat with Freddie, Peter, Cindy and the two St. John-Finneses that first night before dinner.

The room was empty. He looked around, in the hope of spotting some newspapers. None—not even copies of the television guides. There was a television, however, and he took four strides to get to it. The set was dead. Plugged in, switched on at the mains, but dead as a stone. The same applied to the tuner radio facility on the stereo system.

Nothing, it seemed, was coming into Endor through normal means. Bond assumed that any other television or radio would also be inoperable, which signaled a need for him, and possibly the others, to be separated from world events. Cut off. In isolation.

He stayed downstairs for five minutes or so before retracing his steps to his room.

An hour or so later Tigerbalm came, alone, to tell him they were going to have a meal shortly. "The chief says you can join us." He showed no particular feelings for Bond, either friendly or hostile, only the terse, necessary cordiality of a messenger. Somewhere along the morning road Tigerbalm's bouncy bonhomie had dissipated.

The dining room was bare of its good furniture and trappings. In place of the refectory table, a series of functional, military trestle tables had been set up, while the food was collected from another cloth-covered table—soup, bread, cheese, several salad dishes. All very simple with only mineral water to drink.

The room, however, was crowded, and Bond recognized most of the faces from Erewhon. Only Tigerbalm and Happy appeared out of their depth, bulky and furtive among the serious, sunburned, soldierly young men.

"James, good to see you." Simon stood at his elbow.

"I wondered where you'd got to," Bond replied. He studied the face carefully. The openness, so visible at Erewhon, had now turned to camouflage—a change that confirmed the situation every bit as much as the alterations in the decor. Whatever plot, plan or caper had been set in motion by SPECTRE, it was already running. D minus two, three, four or five, Bond reckoned. Then he drastically reduced the odds in his head as he spotted Tamil Rahani, seated on one side of St. John-Finnes, and—guess who?—good old Rolling Joe Zwingli on the other. The three men sat apart from everyone else—alone at a smaller table, and were being served with food by a pair of younger "soldiers." Like the others, the leaders were dressed in uniform khaki slacks and drab green pullovers, their heads bent together as though sitting for a portrait to be titled *The Conspirators.*

For a second Bond's mind drifted off to the surveillance team in the village. Had they noted the comings and goings? Were they aware of the dangerous powers gathered together in this place?

"I said, did you rest well?" Simon was speaking to him.

"Rest? Oh, rest, yes." Bond managed a smile. "I had no option, Simon. You saw to that."

"Security," Simon grinned, answering Bond's last remark. "You know all about security, James. You go to sleep in a hot dusty climate, and wake up in a quiet English village. Come, have some food." Simon began piling salads and cheese onto a plate until Bond had to stop him with a gesture of his hand.

They sat together at the end of one of the longer tables, Simon seeing to it that Bond had his back to the three "brains." Bond watched as his partner took a mouthful of bread and cheese, chewing on it, sucking the juices back into his throat. Every inch a trained soldier, he thought.

"Hallo, Old Bald Eagle's coming your way, James. Looks like he's got orders for you."

Then "Old Bald Eagle"—St. John-Finnes—was leaning over them. "James," his voice took on a quiet, confiding tone, as though trying to calm a tantrum-beleaguered child. "Can you spare an hour or two?"

Bond checked himself from making a fatuous remark, nodded and rose, winking at Simon as he followed his employer. He could feel the eyes of both Rahani and Zwingli on his back as they left.

A young man guarded the stairs down to the laboratory and offices. He did not even signify that he had seen them, almost ostentatiously looking the other way.

"I thought I'd give you a chance to lose the American Revolution to me," Jay Autem said as they began the descent. "It's an easy enough simulation at this level, so we can, perhaps, talk about your plans as we fight. Yes?"

"Whatever you say." Noncommittal, but running the high-speed tape of his plan for getting the EPOC Frequency through his mind.

In the main laboratory area, some drastic rearrangements had also taken place. The largest space was now filled up with collapsible wooden chairs, arranged in rows to give the place the look of some small school assembly hall, or a World War II briefing hut. One modern touch, however: Instead of the expected white screen at the far end, facing the chairs, there was a large television projection screen with Jay Autem Holy's version of the Terror Twelve before it.

Bond could not help seeing the two modern typ-

201

ing chairs nearby, or the big chunky joystick controllers.

A training session had obviously been going on for most of the morning. The Balloon Game? Almost certainly.

Then they were through the office and into the large room with its spotlights and map board of the Eastern coastline of late-eighteenth-century America. There was Boston with Bunker Hill and Breed's Hill to the north, Dorchester Heights jutting out to enclose the harbor, and the townships of Lexington and Concord inland. For no apparent reason, Bond recalled hearing Americans pronounce Concord with a shortened second syllable so that it sounded like Conquered. Jay Autem was smiling down at the board, with its movable open rectangle and all the games paraphernalia set at the two adjacent tables.

Bond saw the smile, and the look, and in that one second abruptly realized that, for all the man's brilliance in his chosen field, the chink in his armor was glaringly obvious.

His interest in strategy and tactics had evolved into an obsession—an obsession with winning; just as his simulations of war, on computer, were his brainchildren only because through them he could beat his own system and win. Like an overindulged child, Dr. Jay Autem Holy was only interested in winning. To lose was the ultimate failure. Had he lost some internal Pentagon battle when he dropped out of life all those years ago? Bond speculated, steeling himself meanwhile, then concentrating on the rapid instructions issued by his Games Master.

Certainly the rules were simple enough. Each player took a turn, which was divided into four phases—Orders; Movement; Challenge; and Resolution. Some of these moves could be made in secret—and, therefore, not seen by the opponent—by marking the location of troops, or matériel, on a small duplicate map of the playing area, a pile of which rested in front of each player. "When we transfer the whole thing onto computer there's an even more ingenious method of making the 'unobserved moves,'" Jason told him, with all the pride of a small boy showing off a collection of toy soldiers.

The playing area itself, on the grid of the large map, was marked out in hundreds of black hexagons. Each side had counters that represented number, strength and type of unit—black for one piece of cannon, with horses and crew; green for five men; blue, ten; red, twenty, and so on. There were also counters overprinted with a horse, denoting mounted troops, while special counters were set out to represent arms caches and leading members of the revolutionary cause.

In good weather men on foot could move five hexes, seven on horseback, and cannon only two. These moves were restricted by bad weather, and by woodland or hills.

Once Orders had been noted, the player moved and then challenged—either by coming within two hexes of an enemy counter, or by declaring that he had sight over five hexes, thereby revealing any "hidden" moves. After the Challenge came the Resolution, in which various strengths, fatigue, weather and so on, were taken into consideration, and the outcome of the Challenge—which could be a skirmish or a full-scale bloody battle—would be noted, one or the other player losing troops, matériel or the action itself.

As each turn, at the beginning, covered a timescale of one day—and the whole episode lasted from September 1774 to June 1775, Bond realized they could be at it for many hours.

"Once we get it onto the computer, the whole business becomes faster, of course," Holy remarked as they both began their Orders phase—with Bond playing the British. He recalled Peter Amadeus' remarks: that his opponent almost expected the British to make the same moves—and mistakes—they had in history.

As Bond recalled it, the garrison commander had been hamstrung by the length of time orders took to reach him from England. Had he acted decisively in the first weeks and months, this opening period could have had a very different outcome. History would have been changed and—while independence would almost certainly have followed at some point—lives, as well as face, might have been saved.

He opened by showing patrols going out of Boston to search the surrounding countryside, but also made secret forays in order to gain control of the high ground—Bunker and Breed's hills, together with Dorchester Heights, at an early stage.

He was surprised to find how, once playing, the game moved much faster than expected.

"The fascination for me," Holy observed as Bond took out two arms caches and around twenty revolutionaries on the Lexington road, "is the juxtaposition of reality and fiction. But, in your former job, this must have been a constant problem."

Bond secretly took three more cannon toward Breed's Hill, a section of thirty men in a final move to the top of Dorchester Heights, while showing more patrols on the ground along the Boston–Concord line. "Yes," he answered, reminding himself to be truthful, "yes, I have lived a fictitious life within a reality—it is the daily bread of field agents."

"I trust you are living in reality now, friend Bond. I say that because what is being planned in this house can also change the course of history." Holy revealed two strong bodies of the colonial militia along the road, attacking the British patrols so fiercely that Bond lost almost twenty men and was forced to withdraw and regroup. Secretly, though, he still poured men, and weapons, onto the dominating ground. The Battle of Bunker Hill—if it ever came—would be completely reversed, with the British forces in a strong and dominant position defending instead of attacking under the withering fire of the entrenched militia.

"One hopes that any change can only be for the good, and that lives are not put at risk."

"Lives are always at risk." The master of Endor found himself losing four caches of weapons and ammunition in a farmhouse on the far side of Lexington, realizing as he did so that Bond had also begun to move his forces on Concord. He shrugged. "But, as for your own life, I know there is no point in threatening you with sudden death. Any threat to your person is of little importance."

"I wouldn't say that," Bond found himself smiling. "We all like life. The thought of being separated from it is as good a lever as any."

The date pages on the calendar easel showed them almost at the end of December, and the weather was against both sides. All either of them could do now was consolidate—openly, or using the clandestine option. Bond decided to divide his forces, encircling the road between Lexington and Concord, while his remaining troops continued to fortify the hills and heights. Holy appeared to be playing a more devious game—sniping at British patrols and, Bond suspected, moving forces toward the high ground already occupied by the British. They played, turn after turn as the weather grew worse and movement was further restricted. Yet throughout this phase, the master of Endor carried on a conversation that appeared to have little to do with the simulated battle.

"Your part in our mission," he took out five of Bond's men, "is of exceptional importance, and you will undoubtedly have to use much fiction, and illusion, to accomplish it."

"Yes. I've been giving it a lot of thought."

"Have you given thought to the way in which governments mislead their gullible peoples?"

"In what way?" he now had sizable forces on all three sections of ground overlooking Boston.

"The obvious, of course, is the so-called balance of power. The United States does not draw attention to the fact that it is outnumbered in space by Russian satellites—not to mention things like the fractional orbital bombing system, in which the Soviets hold a monopoly of seventeen to zero."

"The figures are there for anybody." Bond would soon have to make a serious challenge from the high ground, as colonial forces struggled upward in increasing numbers, restricted by both the climb and the snow.

"Oh, yes, but neither side makes a big thing about figures." Jason scanned the board, brow creased. "Except when Russia takes umbrage at the deployment of Cruise and Pershings in Europe—even when she can more than adequately match them. But James, I may call you James? What is the real conspiracy here? The British tie up many policemen against antinuclear protesters. Yet nobody says to these well-meaning people, 'If it happens, brothers and sisters—which it will not—it's not going to happen with a big nuclear bang. The Cruise and Pershing are for rattling only. What could occur will be ten thousand times worse.'"

"Nobody tells the protesters in the United States, either." Bond watched as his opponent edged even larger numbers of men toward the waiting British guns and fought a small skirmish along the constant battlefront of the country between Boston and Concord.

"And yet, if it came, James, what *would* happen?"

"Your guess is as good as mine. Certainly not the big bang and mushroom cloud. More like the bright lights, and a very nasty chemical cloud."

"Quite—I challenge from this hex," his arm moved out, to an area between Concord and Lexington, where British troops were now much thinner on the ground. "No, it will be neutrons and chemicals. A lot of death, but little destruction—then a Mexican stand-off in space, with the Soviets holding the big stick up there."

"Unless the United States and the NATO forces have done something to equalize things. That's what's going on, isn't it?" Why this? Bond asked himself. Why this chatter about the balance of power, and the place nuclear weapons played in that balance? Why talk of this to me?

Then he recalled the sound advice always given in classes on interrogation—don't listen to the words, let your ears hear the music. The orchestration makes the banal words seem more intelligent; the clever, soaring strings took your mind from the cheap potency of simple, emotional ideas.

It was late January, and, at a challenge, Bond had to reveal there were British forces ringing the far side of Concord. Holy started to cut them apart with his colonial militia, sniping across the winter landscape. Readily, Bond saw how addictive this kind of exercise could become. Using imagination, one could almost feel the cold and fatigue that played havoc with men's strength and fighting ability. One even heard the crack of musket fire, and saw the blood staining the dirty snow in some farmer's field.

Holy was not really talking about the lopsided balance of power. He was talking about the need to end the whole system that controlled that balance.

"Would the world not really be a better, and safer, place if the real strength was removed? If the stings were drawn from the superpowers' tails?" he asked, making another foray into the bleak Massachusetts winter scene.

"If it was possible, yes," Bond agreed. "It would be better, but I doubt safer. Slingshot or nuclear weapon, the world's always been dangerous." One more turn and he would have to declare his presence in the hills.

Jay Autem Holy leaned back, temporarily stopping play. "We're involved in halting the race to the holocaust—nuclear, neutron or chemical. To you is entrusted the task of getting that EPOC Frequency. Now, do you yet have a way?" As though he did not expect an answer, he played through his turn, concentrating on bringing men well into the British zone of fire.

"I have the makings of a plan. It will require certain information in advance . . ."

"What kind of information?"

"When you need the Frequency, I shall have to know, a little ahead of time, exactly who the Duty Security Officer is, for the night in question, at the Foreign Office . . ."

"That presents no problem. One man does the job for a whole week, yes?"

"As a rule."

"And he is a senior officer?"

Bond spread the fingers of his right hand, making a rocking movement. "Let's say middle management."

"But you are likely to know him?"

"That's why I really have to get a name. If you can't provide it, then I shall have to telephone."

"We can provide."

"Then, if I know him, I shall still have to make a

210

call. If he is unknown to me—unlikely but possible—
I'll have to think again."

"If you know him . . . ?"

"I have a way of getting in. I should only need an
hour, at the most, in his company." Bond prayed it
would work. "I challenge you here," his finger
hovered around the upper reaches of Breed's Hill.

"But . . ." his opponent began, then realized the
trap that Bond had sprung.

A few minutes later, as he faced slaughter on the
slopes of Bunker Hill, having lost the majority of his
men and arms on Dorchester Heights and Breed's
Hill, Jay Autem angrily told Bond that he would have
plenty of warning. "You'll *know* who the officer is.
That I promise you!" He watched as Bond revealed
two more cannon to counterattacking militia on the
far side of the hill. "This is the wrong way round," he
said, barely controlling his rage. "And Bunker Hill
can't happen until June—it's hardly February!"

"And this is the fiction," Bond answered calmly,
feeling a measure of satisfaction in spite of himself.
"The reality's history—even though a great deal of
history happens to be fiction also."

Then, suddenly, the storm broke. Jay Autem
Holy's chest seemed to swell, and his cheeks went
crimson. "You . . . You . . . You . . ." The voice rising
to a scream. "You've beaten me! ME!" One huge
hand swept the papers from his playing area, then
descended in a fist. "How dare you? How dare you

even . . ." It was an awesome rage as the man spluttered. He stamped his feet; he literally kicked the table. Awesome, and yet funny, as a child's tantrums are amusing yet distressing.

Then, as suddenly as the rage had begun, it stopped. There was no dusk, no twilight, for sanity appeared to return, and Holy stood, looking for a brief moment like a chastened child.

"The militia could rally yet," the voice small, throaty. "But we've played too long," with a wave of the hand, "I have other things to do. Better things."

He stood, as though winning or losing a game were now of little consequence to him. When he spoke, the tone was completely normal, as if nothing unusual had taken place. "The object of spending this time with you, though, was to hear how your thoughts were shaping up—regarding your part in the operation." Quiet and conversational, making it all the more bizarre. "Tell me, if you happen to know the man on duty, how do you propose to get the Frequency from him?"

Bond, who was amazed to see by his watch that it was already eight in the evening, began to recite the method he had mentally prepared. Silence stretched out—the hush in the aftermath of a battle fought with counters instead of men, and on a board and map instead of ground. No reaction. As the seconds ticked by, he thought perhaps there had been a miscalculation. He sifted through his mind. Was there any really weak point? Anything that Jay Autem Holy could grab at to prove the whole idea a mere insubstantial fiction—which it surely was?

Then the silence ended, and a laugh began to rise from the tall man's throat, the head nodding in great beaky movements, as if preparing to tear his prey apart, savaging it with that sharp bill.

"Oh, yes, James Bond. I told them you were the only possible choice. If you can pull that off we'll *all* be happy, not that . . ."

He broke off suddenly, appearing to pull himself together, eyes darting around, as though he had been on the brink of an indiscretion.

The laughter subsided, and Bond was aware of movement. People were entering the main laboratory area.

"We have been down here for too long," Jay Autem snapped. "I took the trouble to ask Cindy to make up a tray for you. In your room. I shall eat later."

Superman, thought Bond. He's telling me that he's a survivor. Go without food and drink for long periods. "In the desert," he said softly, "when you were with General Zwingli—after you jumped from that airplane—did you have to go long without food and drink?"

The green eyes went bitterly cold, all sign of normal human life ebbing from them.

"Clever, Mr. Bond. How long have you known?"

213

Realizing that he had overplayed his hand, and not really certain why he had done so, Bond said he had suspected it from their first meeting. "It just happened that I'd read the old file. They resurrect it from time to time, you know. I thought I knew your face the moment we met—when I came here with Freddie. During the evening, I became more convinced, but still not one hundred percent sure. After all, if you *are* Jay Autem Holy, you've been dead a long time."

"And what if you had still been on active service, Mr. Bond? Would you have gone running to your superiors? And why, incidentally, is the file resurrected regularly?"

"You know what the Colonial militia is like," Bond tried to inject humor into his voice. "*Your* Colonial militia. They jump at ghosts. Spooks."

Jay Autem made a growling noise. "Tamil was right. It's a pity we didn't pull you in sooner. His people tried, against my advice. You see, I did not wish to deal with yet another hostage; another woman—you had some woman with you, yes? Anyway, the job was bungled; you were quick, and used cunning. So." The tense atmosphere changed yet again. There were no advance warnings with Holy. "Well, I have work to do. You stand by, James, and thank heaven we have you now."

They were gathering in the main laboratory, all young and bronzed—except Tigerbalm and Happy.

214

Bond saw that Zwingli was still in deep conversation with Tamil Rahani, as though they had not stopped since lunch.

"Just see Mr. Bond up the stairs," Holy spoke to Tigerbalm, giving Bond a small pat on the shoulder, as if reassuring himself that all was well.

Tigerbalm went as far as the landing and watched as Bond walked to his room. He recalled being told that, appearances to the contrary, Jay Autem was a genius of sorts—was it Percy who had told him? The man obviously lived in that odd world of unreality. If he said he was dead, then that was exactly what the world should believe. Holy had been genuinely shaken by the idea that others might not be convinced. Then there was the question of Percy—"You had some woman with you, yes?" Well, who was it who had said that not even Holy would recognize his own wife?

He opened the door, and there—for the second time—was Cindy Chalmer, a finger of one hand to her lips, a hard computer disk clutched in the other.

Bond closed the door. "More greetings from Percy?" he asked softly.

– 15 –

The Balloon Game

"No. This one's on me." She saw the look in Bond's eye, and followed his gaze, for he had suddenly become hesitant, wary, moving quietly around the room.

Softly she spoke again, "It's okay, James. They have visual surveillance, and a superabundance of military detection gear, but this lot don't seem to have caught up with the all-powerful bug."

"You certain?" he mouthed.

"Swept the place myself. In my first week; and I've kept abreast of all the security developments since. If they've put any sound in, I'll turn back into a virgin."

Bond nodded. There was nothing to be amused about now. Even though he appeared satisfied, throughout the time they were together in the room all conversation was conducted in a low murmur. Foolish, he thought, for that would be as audible to sophisticated equipment as yelling should Cindy be proved wrong.

"The Balloon Game." She held out the hard disk to him, a small flat square encased in plastic.

So she had got it, stored away on the wafer-thin magnetic disk, the program that would provide the answer to what SPECTRE had proposed to Rahani and Holy. Yet he did not move to take it from her.

"Well, don't just stand there. At least say thank you."

He remained silent, wishing to draw her out. The trick was as old as the trade itself, practiced constantly by case officers and agent handlers the world over. Remain silent and let them come to you, tell you all there is to tell.

"They've got four backup copies," she said at last, "and I just hope to heaven the Old Bald Eagle doesn't need to run the fourth, 'cause this is it."

"I thought they'd buried it, locked it behind steel and sprinkled man-eating spiders in the vault." He still did not smile.

"The original, and its backups, have been kept in the chief's safe—the one in his office that does have everything except the man-eating spiders." Once more she held it out. "But today it's all systems go, and they're using it all the time. As often happens,

Peter and I have been banished from the lab. But the guards have got used to us going up and down. You beat him at his own game, I gather?"

"Yes." As though there had been no pleasure in it.

"Heard some of it. Now perhaps you'll believe he's insane—had one of his tantrums. Heard that as well."

"How did you get down?"

"Looked as though I belonged. Clipboard under one arm. They've seen me before. I just walked past the young thugs on the door. You were with Bald Eagle. Like a lot of people who become paranoid about security, he has a blind spot. The safe was left open. I did a swift switch, and tucked this up my shirt."

It was all he was going to get. "You haven't seen it run, then?"

She shook her head. Her negative gestures, he noticed, were always performed with the head tilted slightly to the right—a distinctive mannerism—a flourish, like the way some people curl the last letter of their signature, underlining the name to give it more importance. It was a habit they should have caught during training where the mohair-suited psychiatrists note, and expunge, mannerisms. He waited again.

"There's been no way, James. Only the inner circle've seen it, played with it—if that's the right word."

At last Bond took the disk. "Trained on it," he

corrected. "And there's little chance of us having a look-see. My gear's where exactly?"

"In the garage. Under a pile of rubbish—tires, old tins, tools. In one corner. I had to improvise, and it was better to hide it there than let them find it in the car. It's not safe by any means, so we just have to hope nobody goes rooting around."

He seemed to give the situation a lot of thought. Then said, "Well, I for one don't fancy trying to unlock this," he touched the disk. "What's on it is big, and, I suspect, exceptionally dangerous. I just hope you're right—that the disk isn't missed, and that nobody goes rooting through the garage."

"So what good's it going to do? You want me to try and get it out?"

He walked over to the window, where the chintz Laura Ashley curtains had been drawn. The promised supper tray was on a table nearby, and he noticed it had been set for two—prawns in little glasses, cold chicken and tongue, salads; a bottle of wine; bread rolls. Did anybody get hot food at Endor when the heat was on? he wondered. Then he started thinking about the disk, still clutched in his hand. Better if he kept it close. Yet there were few really possible hiding places. In the end, he banked on there being no search, walked over to the wardrobe and stuck it among his clothes.

"There are friends," he confided at last. "Quite near. I would have thought that by now . . . No, you

220

don't move from the house. Nobody tries to get out except me." Bond turned, and dropped quietly into a chair, signaling she should also sit. He nodded toward the wardrobe. "No risks, not with that. It's like a time bomb."

Cindy perched on the end of the bed, her skirt riding up to show a slice of smooth thigh. "We just sit, and wait until the cavalry arrive?"

"Something like that." He was thinking, trying to reckon what time they might have; whether the surveillance team, with their cameras, log books, directional microphones and all their other Boy's Book of Spies gear had advised M that something major was imminent. Would M sweat it out? Possibly. The cautious, diplomatic intriguer had waited before—until the very last moment.

"I want an educated guess from you, Cindy. You've been here before—I mean when they've prepared for some caper . . . ?"

Okay, she had been at Endor when the hard men came and spent hours down in the converted cellars, training.

"This is the biggest gathering yet?"

Since she had been here it was. Yes.

"In your estimation, Cindy, what's the timing? How long've we got before things start to roll?" In his mind the question was really, how long have *I* got before they ask me to filch the EPOC Frequency?

"It can only be a guess, but I'd say forty-eight hours, max."

"And your little playmate, Peter . . . ?"

She sprang to Peter's defense, like a sister. "Peter is okay. He's a brilliant worker, dedicated . . ."

"Would you trust him? Really trust, when the chips are down, as they say?"

She gnawed her upper lip. Only in a real emergency. Nothing against him; he couldn't stand the boss. "He's been looking for a different job. Says this place is too claustrophobic for him."

"I expect it's going to be even more claustrophobic. That you, Peter and myself are destined for oblivion. Anybody who isn't completely in their confidence." Once more he stayed silent, for nearly a full minute, his mind slicing through every morsel of information. Jay Autem had indicated that SPECTRE's current ploy was destined to change history. If it wasn't just some outrageous piece of stupidity, then it was quite possible the evil organization had latched on to something earth-shattering. Afterward, they would not want anybody around who could name names, or draw faces. Certainly not in the immediate wake of whatever they planned.

"My car," he began.

"The Bentley? Yes?"

"You took my gear from the boot. How?"

It was just before the present crowd arrived. Cindy had been through the kitchens and spotted large amounts of food being loaded into the two big deep freezes. She had also heard Old Bald Eagle on the telephone. "I knew they were bringing you back. What did happen, by the way? They said you were in hospital . . ."

Bond brusquely told her to get on with it.

She knew the car had been driven back and put into the garage, and she wondered about the micro and drives he had used in the hotel. The Bentley's keys were left in a security cabinet ("Where they keep all the car keys. I've been in and out of that one since I first arrived.") and she chose her moment.

"It was a risk, but I only had the keys out for five minutes. Everyone was busy, so I took the keys, unloaded the boot and stashed the stuff in the garage. It's not a hundred percent safe, but it seemed to be the only way. Bad enough doing that, and far too risky to attempt getting it any further away."

"And the car itself? Have they done anything with it? Gone over it?"

She gave her angled negative head shake. "No time. Not enough troops either."

"The keys?"

"Jason'll have them."

"And it's still there? In the garage?"

"Far as I know. Why?"

"Can we . . . ?"

"Forget it, James. There's no way we can drive out of here in one piece."

"I hope to be going officially. But, if they haven't messed about with it, I wouldn't mind spending fifteen minutes in that car now. Possible?"

"The keys? . . . How? . . . Lord, I don't . . ."

"Don't worry about keys. Just tell me, Cindy, can we get into the garage?"

"Well, I can." She explained that her room had a window looking out on the garage roof. "You just drop down, and there's a skylight. Opens upward. No problem."

"And security?"

"Damn. Yes, they've got a couple of young guys out front." She explained the layout. The garage itself held four cars, and was, in effect, an extension to the north end of the house. Her room was on the corner, just above the flat roof—one window looking down on the garage, two more to the front.

"And these guards? They're out front? Specifically watching the garage?"

"Just general duties. Keeping an eye on the north end. If we could . . . wait a minute. If my curtains aren't drawn they can see straight up into my room. I caught one lot at it last night. They just move a shade farther down the drive and they have a good view. How would it be if I gave them a peep show?"

Bond smiled for the first time. "Well, I'd appreciate it."

Cindy leaned back on the bed. "You, James, you

224

male chauvinist pig, have the opportunity to appreciate it any time you want: and that's an offer."

"Which I'd love to take up, Cindy. But we have
work. Let's see how good they've been with my luggage." He went over to the weekend case and
dumped it on the bed beside the girl, then knelt to
examine the locks. After a few seconds he nodded
and took out the black gunmetal pen, unscrewing the
wrong end to reveal a tiny set of miniature screw-
driver heads. In turn, these were threaded at their
blunt ends, the threads matching a small hole in the
pen's cap. "No traveler should be without one," Bond
smiled, selecting one of the drivers, and screwing it
into place.

He then carefully started to remove the tiny
screws around the right lock of his case. They turned
easily, the lock coming off in one piece to reveal a
small oblong cavity containing one spare set of keys
for the Mulsanne Turbo, which he slipped into his
pocket, before replacing the lock, and putting away
the miniature tool kit.

The plans—for Cindy's diversion, and Bond's
crawl from her window—were quickly arranged. "Diversion's no problem," she said, lowering her lids,
"I've got exceptional quality tart's stuff on under the
skirt." A small pout. "Thought I might even turn you
on." She outlined her room, suggesting that she
should enter in the dark, open the side window—with

its drop onto the garage roof—and pull those curtains before switching the light on. "I'll be able to see exactly where the guards have placed themselves, and you'll have to crawl to the side window on your belly."

"How long can you . . . Well, tantalize them?"

If she performed the full act, Cindy said, putting on a throaty voice, she could keep them more or less happy for an hour. "To be on the safe side, I guess about ten minutes, give or take five."

He gave her a look reserved usually for the more cheeky jumpers and pearls set at the Regent's Park Office, checked the ASP, and said the sooner they got on with it, the better. Bond's common sense told him that, if they had not yet tampered with the car, it would certainly be given a going over before they let him out—*if* they let him out—to perform his allotted task.

Nobody appeared to be stirring in the house. The men still lounged in the hall—they saw them tiptoeing across the landing, but the rest was quiet, and the corridor leading to Cindy's room, at the far end of the house, was in darkness. Her smooth palm touched his, their fingers interlocking for a moment as she guided him toward her door.

She was young, supple, very attractive, and obviously available—to him at least. For a second he wondered, not for the first time, how genuine she was. But that option of trust had long since passed. There was nobody else.

226

Cindy opened her door, whispering, "Okay, down boy." He dropped onto his stomach, beginning to wiggle across the floor. Cindy was humming to herself, and interspersing the low tuneful bluesy sound with soft comments, "Nobody at the side . . . I'm closing the curtains . . . Okay, going to the front windows . . . Yes, they're down there . . . Right, James, get cracking, I'm putting the lights on . . ." And on they flooded, with Bond halfway across the floor, moving fast toward the window, in front of which the curtains billowed and sighed like a sail.

As he reached it, he saw her out of the corner of his eye, standing near the far front window, hands to her shirt, swaying slightly as she sang softly:

> He shakes my ashes, freezes my griddle,
> Churns my butter, stokes my pillow
> My man is such a handyman.
>
> He threads my needle, gleans my wheat,
> Heats my heater, chops my meat,
> My man is such a handyman.

The last words were barely distinguishable to Bond, who was out of the window, dropping silently onto the garage roof, by then.

Flat against the roof, his body pressing down as if to merge with the lead surface, Bond let his eyes adjust to the darkness. Then he froze, hearing first the noise of feet on gravel—to his left, at the front of the house—then the voices, alerted.

They spoke in heavily accented English, and there were, as Cindy had said, two of them.

One made a hushing sound. Then—

"What?"

"The roof. Didn't you hear it?"

"A noise? What?"

"Sounded like someone on the garage roof . . ."

Bond tried to will his body into the flat surface, pressing down, his head turned away, heart thudding in his ears.

"On the roof? No."

"Move back. Take a look. You know what he said—no second chances."

The feet on the gravel again.

"I can't see any . . ."

"You think we should go and . . . ?"

Bond's hand inched toward the ASP.

"There's nobody there. No . . . Hey, look at that!" The scuffle of feet moving back off the gravel.

Bond turned his head, and saw the clear silhouettes of the two guards below, in front of the house. They were close to one another, looking up like a pair of astronomers studying a new planet, eyes fixed on the windows out of his line of vision.

Carefully he started to move over the roof toward its center, where he knew the skylight lay. Then, suddenly, flat again as the guards also moved—his own breathing sounding violently loud, as though it would draw everyone to him. But the two men were now backing away from the house, heads tilted, trying to get a better view—a clearer angle—on what was happening just inside Cindy's lighted, open window.

Again he edged forward, going as fast as safety would allow, conscious of each minute slipping away.

The skylight moved at his first touch. Very gently he slid it back, staring down into the darkness below.

They had made it easier for him by parking the gray Mercedes directly underneath. One swing and he was down, feet on the car's roof, head less than a foot below the edge of the skylight.

Bond slipped the ASP from its holster. Once more he waited, stock still, letting eyes adjust and ears strain. No sound, except the beating of his own heart, no sign of any movement, but certainly the long outline of the Mulsanne Turbo parked to his right.

He dropped to the floor, one hand still grasping the ASP, the other now clutching the keys.

The lock of the Bentley thumped open, and there was that solid, satisfying sound as the catch gave way to his thumb and the heavy door swung back.

He slid into the driving seat and checked the connections around the Super 1000 long-range telephone, which Communications Control Systems had provided for the electronics wizards of Rolls-Royce to wire in. Then he picked up the handset, letting out a breath of relief as the small pin of red light came on to signify the telephone was active. His one fear had been that Jay Autem's or Tamil Rahani's men had cut the connections. Now, all he could do was pray nobody was monitoring the closed waveband.

Quickly he punched out the number, and, before the distant end had time to say "Transworld Exports," he rasped out, "Predator! Confuse!" hitting the small blue scramble button as he said it, then counting to twenty, waiting for the distant to come up again.

"Confused!" the voice of the duty officer at the Regent's Park Headquarters said clearly.

"I say this once only. Predator, emergency," and Bond launched into a fast two-minute message that he hoped would cover all the angles if Jay Autem Holy really intended to send him out from Endor to steal the United States EPOC Frequency within the next few days.

Putting the telephone back into its cradle, between the seats, he retrieved the ASP, which had rested only a cobra-strike from his hand, above the polished wooden dashboard, and returned it to the holster.

Now he had to make it back to Cindy's room as fast as possible. The thought of the girl slowly stripping, singing to herself, was highly erotic, but his mind flitted to other thoughts—about Percy Proud, to his passing surprise. A trick of the subconscious, he

230

decided, closing the Bentley's door as quietly as its weight allowed, and operating the locking system.

He had just turned, to head back to the Mercedes, when a sharp double metallic click brought him to a halt.

There was an old game—from back in World War II—which they still played in training courses. You sat in darkness while tapes of noises were run. The object was to identify each noise. Often it was the distinctive cocking action of an automatic pistol (in training they ran this with sounds of door handles, toys, even metal snap fastenings). The sharp double click that he heard now came from the far side of the Mercedes, and Bond would know it anywhere. It was the automatic pistol.

The ASP was in his hand again, but as the gun came up, so the spotlight flashed on, and a familiar voice spoke softly:

"Put that nasty thing away, dear. It's not really worth it, and neither of us wants to get hurt, do we?"

– 16 –
EPOC

BOND COULD SEE HIM quite clearly, outlined against the lighter coloring of the wall. In a fraction of a second, his brain and body calculated the situation and made a decision.

Normally, with all his training and the long built-in reflexes, Bond would have taken him out with one shot—probably straight from the hip. But several factors intervened.

The voice was not aggressive, denoting room for barter; the words had been plain, simple and to the point—"neither of us wants to get hurt, do we?"—and, most important, there was no noise-reduction system fitted to the ASP. A shot, from either side, would bring unwanted company into the garage. Bond's reactions concluded that Peter was as anxious as himself to keep the wolves at bay.

"Okay, Peter. What's the score?" Almost a whisper, as Peter Amadeus came closer. Bond sensed, more than saw, that the small pistol, just visible, held away from the body, was moving around like a tree in a gale. The precise little man was very nervous.

"The score, Mr. Bond, is that I want out—and as far away from here as possible. I gathered from your one-way talkabout that you're thinking of going as well."

"I'm going when I'm told—by your boss and the others. Do they know you're out, by the way?"

"If the gods happen to be on my side, they won't notice. If the hue and cry is raised, I just pray they won't come looking here."

"Peter, you won't get out at all unless I go back the way I came pretty damned quickly. Wouldn't it be better for you to stay put?"

The pistol sagged in Amadeus' hand, and this time his voice edged one notch toward hysteria. "I can't, Mr. Bond! I can't do it. The place, those people—particularly Bald Eagle . . . I just can't stay in the house any longer!"

"Right," Bond soothed, hoping the young man's voice would not rise too high. "If we can think of a way, would you give evidence if necessary? Make a clear statement?"

"I've got the best evidence in the world," he

seemed calmer, on safer ground. "I've seen it run—The Balloon Game; I know what it's about, and that's enough to terrify any red-blooded man, let alone me."

"What? Tell me."

"You haven't got time, and it's my only ace. You get me out, and I'll give any help you may need. Deal?"

"I can't promise." Bond was acutely aware that time was slipping by. Cindy would not be able to distract the two guards much longer. He told Peter to put the gun away, going very close to him now. "If they're letting me out, to do a bit of their dirty work, it's pretty certain they'll go through the Bentley with the finest of toothcombs. You've also got to realize that your absence puts a lot of people at risk."

"I know, but . . ."

"Okay, it's done now. Listen, and listen carefully . . ." As quickly as he could, Bond instructed Amadeus on the best way of hiding under the other cars in the garage. Then he pressed the keys into the young man's hand. "You only use these *after* they've played around with the Bentley. It's a risk. Anything could happen, and I haven't any assurance they'll even let me go in my own car. One other thing. If you're found here, you get no help—I deny you completely. Right?"

Amadeus, Bond said, should hide in the boot after the car had been examined. Then there was a final instruction should all else fail, or if he, himself, was prevented from going.

Time had just about run out. He patted the little programer's shoulder, wishing him luck, then climbed back onto the Mercedes, hauled himself up through the skylight, and back to the flat roof.

Lying in the chill night air, pressed hard against the lead, he realized that Cindy had exhausted her repertoire. The guards were very close, just below the garage roof. He could hear them muttering—making comments about what they had seen.

He lay, tense and listening, for around five minutes until they moved away, following their routine pattern of covering the front of the house from all angles.

It took a good ten minutes for Bond to snake his way back to the window. After each move he stopped, lying still, ears cocked against the guards, who passed under the garage twice during his uncomfortable crawl. At last he negotiated the sill, climbing back into Cindy's room.

"You took your time."

She was stretched out on the bed, her dark body glistening, the gorgeous long legs moving as she rubbed thigh against thigh. Cindy was quite naked, and Bond, with the tension released, went to her.

"Thank you. I've done all I can."

He was going to say something about Amadeus, but changed his mind—sufficient to the day.

Abruptly Cindy lifted her arms to his shoulders, and Bond, with no power to resist, let himself be dragged down. Only once, as he entered her, did Percy's face and body flash through his head—a picture so vivid that he thought he could smell her particular scent—before these too vanished in the swirling whirlpool.

It was almost dawn when he crept back to his own room, and the house was still silent, as though sleeping in preparation for action. He ate some of the food, threw more down the lavatory, and flushed three times to clear it away. Then at last he lay down on his own bed, still fully dressed, and dropped into a refreshing sleep.

At the first noise he was awake, the right hand reaching for the ASP.

It was Cindy. She carried a breakfast tray, and was followed by Tigerbalm, who smiled his inane grin, saying that Professor St. John-Finnes wished to see him at noon. "That's sharp midday," he added. "I'll come up and fetch yer."

"Please do." Bond moved on the bed, but Cindy was already halfway out the door.

"Cindy," he called.

She did not even look back, "Have a nice day," flung over her shoulder, not unpleasant, but peremptory.

Bond shrugged, worried a little, and then began

to help himself to black coffee and toast. It was ten-thirty by his watch. By eleven-forty-five he was show-ered, shaved and changed, thinking as he went through his routine that even M could not leave it much longer before moving against Endor.

At three minutes to twelve, Tigerbalm reap-peared, and they went downstairs to the rear of the house, where Jay Autem Holy awaited him in a small room he had never seen before.

There was a table, two chairs and a telephone. No pictures, windows or distractions of any kind. The room was lit by two long neon strips, and Bond saw immediately that the chairs and table were bolted to the floor. It was familiar ground: an interrogation room.

"Come in, friend Bond," the head came up in a swooping movement, the green eyes piercing, hostile as laser gun sights. He told Tigerbalm to leave, mo-tioning for Bond to sit down. Then Holy wasted no time.

"The plan you outlined to me—the way of getting your eyes on the current EPOC Frequency . . ."

"Yes."

"It is imperative that we have the Frequency that comes into operation at midnight tonight—covering the next two days."

"I can but . . ."

"You will do more than any buts, James. Our prin-cipals—SPECTRE—are still, the way it turns out, most unhappy about using you. They have sent you a message, which I am to deliver, alone."

Bond waited. A pause of around three beats.

"Those who speak for SPECTRE say that you already know they are not squeamish. They also say that it is useless for us to threaten you personally with death, or anything else—if you do not carry out orders to the letter." He gave the ghost of a smile. "I happen to believe that you're with us, all the way. If you're doubling, then I'd have to admit you've fooled me. However, just so that we all know where we stand, I am to tell you the worst that can happen."

Again Bond did not reply, or allow any change in his expression.

"The operation to which we are all now committed has peaceful aims—I must stress this. True, it will alter history; certainly it will bring about some chaos; there will undoubtedly be resistance from reactionaries. But the change will come, and with it Peace. With a capital P."

"So?"

"So, the EPOC Frequency is a prerequisite to this peaceful solution embedded within SPECTRE's operation. If all goes well, and the very simplicity of the idea appeals to me, there will be little or no bloodshed. If anyone is hurt, it will be the fault of those trying to make a stand against the inevitable.

"What I am instructed to tell you is that, should you fail us, or try any tricks to foil what cannot be foiled, the operation will still go ahead, but the accent on peaceful solutions will be changed. Without the EPOC Frequency there is one way only—the way of horror, terror and the ultimate holocaust."

"I . . ." Bond began, stopped short by Holy's glare.

"They wish me to make it clear to you that, should you be tempted to cut and run, not provide the Frequency, or—worse—try to alter it, then the blood, death, ravage of millions will be on your head, and yours alone. They are not joking, James. We have worked for them now. We have come to know them. To tell you the truth, they terrify me."

"Do they terrify Rolling Joe as well?"

"He's a tough old bird." Holy relaxed a little. "A tough, but disillusioned, old bird. But, yes, they also frighten him." He spread his hands on the table, near the telephone, palms down. "Joe Zwingli lost all faith in his country, roughly at the same time that I came to the conclusion that the United States had become a degenerate, self-serving nation, led by corrupt men. I deduced that America—like Britain—could never be altered from the inside. It had to be done from without. Together we cooked up the idea of disappearing, of working for a truly democratic society, and world peace, from the obscurity of . . . what shall I call it? . . . the obscurity of the grave?"

"How about the obscurity of a whited sepulcher?"

240

The green eyes hardened, diamonds reflecting light. "Not worthy, James. Not if you're with us."

"I was thinking it was what the world might say." Too late, Bond checked his impulse to be less than friendly with the scientist.

"The world will be a very different place within the next forty-eight hours. Few will be concerned with what I did. Many will look with hope to what I have made possible."

"So I go tonight? If you've decided my ploy's the best?"

"You go tonight, and you set things in motion before you go. The Duty Security Officer's name is Denton—Anthony Denton."

"Good."

"You know him?"

In fact, Bond knew Tony Denton well. They had done some courses together in the past and, a few years ago, had been on a bring-'em-back-alive trip— a defector who had walked into the Embassy in Helsinki. Yes, he knew good old Tony Denton, though it would make no difference at all if his instructions had been taken to heart at the Regent's Park Headquarters.

"He goes on duty at six in the evening, I understand," Holy prompted.

Bond said that certainly used to be the old routine; and Holy suggested he should make the telephone call at about six-thirty. "In the meantime, I suspect you'd better get some rest. If you do the job properly, as you *must,* we can all look to a brighter future—to those broad, sunlit uplands of which a great statesman once spoke."

"I go in my own car." He was not asking but telling Holy.

"If you insist. I shall have to instruct that the telephone be disconnected—but you'll not object to that."

"Just leave me an engine and complete set of wheels."

Holy allowed himself the glint of a smile. Then the face hardened again. "James . . ." Bond knew suddenly that he was going to say something unpleasant.

"James, I'm giving you the benefit of the doubt. I understand the nubile Miss Chalmer was in your room last night, furthermore that you were in hers until the early hours. I must ask you, did Cindy Chalmer give you anything? Or try to pass something to you?"

"I trust not," he began, then realized this was not the time for facetious remarks. "No. Nothing. Should she have?"

Holy stared at the table. "She says not. Idiot girl. Sometime yesterday she removed what she imagined to be a rather important computer program from the laboratory. She's shown signs of willfulness before

242

now, so I personally set a small trap for her. The program she stole was rubbish, quite worthless. She says that you knew nothing of her action, and I'm inclined to believe her. But the fact remains that she hid the disk among your clothes—where, James, it has been found. Cindy made quite a speech about it. She seems to have concluded that we're—as she puts it—up to no good. So she took the disk, as some kind of evidence, and hid the thing in your room until she could think of some way to use it against me." He became hesitant. "We've kept it in the family, James—by which I mean that we've not let it go beyond Dazzle and myself. My partners—Rahani and Zwingli—could become alarmed, might pass it on to the representatives of SPECTRE. I don't think we'd want that, would we? A domestic problem. None of their business."

So, thought Bond, as serious a matter as stealing even a dummy backup program of The Balloon Game—on which, he presumed, the whole operation for SPECTRE was based—could be overlooked and kept "in the family." It was an interesting turn of events. One thing it suggested was that Jay Autem Holy lived in fear of SPECTRE; and that was a piece of deduction that might well be put to valuable use later.

"Cindy?" Bond mused. "What . . . ?"

"Will happen to her? She is regarded as one of my family. She will be disciplined—like a child—and kept very close, under guard, lock and key. Dazzle is seeing to it."

"I haven't seen your wife recently."

"Dazzle? No, she prefers to remain in the background. But she has certain tasks to perform, tasks necessary to success. What I really wish to ask of you, James, is that we keep this business about Miss Chalmer to ourselves. Keep it as a personal matter. I mean, we don't mention it to anybody. Personal, between us, eh?"

"Personal," Bond echoed, keeping his thoughts to himself. What else was there to say?

Tigerbalm came for him shortly after six o'clock. They had not locked him in, though food was served on a tray, brought up by a young Arab.

They went to the same room as before—with its bolted-down table and chairs. The only difference this time was that a tape recorder, with a separate set of earphones, had been hooked up to the telephone.

"It's time, then." Holy was not alone. Tamil Rahani stood beside him, while the large, craggy face of Rolling Joe Zwingli peered out from behind them.

"I can't promise this part will work," Bond said, his voice flat and calm. So calm that it appeared to activate something within General Zwingli, who pushed his way through his partners, sticking out a leathery hand.

244

"We haven't met, Commander Bond." The voice had a slightly Texan tang to it. "My name's Joe Zwingli, and I just want to wish you luck. Get in there and *make* it happen for us, Commander. It's in a great cause—to put your country and mine back on their feet."

Bond did not want to disillusion the man. Heaven knew, the day SPECTRE did anything that was not for their own good would be, he reckoned, the first day of never. He played it, however, to the hilt.

"I'll do what I can, sir," he said, then he sat down, waited for Holy to ready the tape monitor, don the headphones and indicate they were set.

He picked up the handset and punched out the digits, which, or so he had led them to believe, would access the special small complex where the SIS Duty Security Officer to the Foreign Office spent his twelve-hour watches, together with specialist tele-printer, cipher, radio and computer operators. In fact, the number he punched was a screened tele-phone number known only to the field officers of his Service. It was also manned day and night, and hid many identities—depending upon what operations were being run.

That night it was a Chinese laundry based in Soho; a radio cab firm; a French restaurant; and—if the matter arose—the Foreign Office Duty Security Officer's direct line. For that purpose it had been alerted for special action ever since Bond's flash radiophone call from the garaged Bentley, the previous evening. If the call came, it would be passed to one person only.

It rang four times, before anyone picked it up. "Hallo?" The voice was flat.

"Tony Denton, please—the DO, please."

"Who wants him?"

"Predator." He saw Holy give a wry smile, for, when outlining his plan, Bond had refused to give the last cryptonym he had used as a member of the Service. Apparently Jay Autem Holy thought this one very apt.

"Hang on, please." They were switching the call through to the instrument near wherever Bill Tanner was currently situated, and it was his old friend Tanner's voice that next sounded in Bond's ear.

"Denton. I thought you were out, Predator? This is an irregular call, which I really must terminate."

"Tony! Wait!" Bond hunched over the table. "This is priority. Yes, I'm out—as far as anyone can be out—but I have something vital to the Service. But *really* vital."

"Go on." Unconvinced.

"Not on the phone. Not safe. You're the only person I could think of. I must see you. I *have* to see you. Imperative, Tony. Consul." He used the standard cipher word for extreme emergency.

At the far end there was a fractional pause. "When?"

"Tonight. Certainly before midnight. I can get to you, I think. Please, Tony, give me the all-clear."

Again the deep, breathless pause. "If this isn't straight I'll see you in West End Central, and in Court by morning, charged under the Official Secrets Act. As quickly as you can. I'll clear you. Right?"

"Be with you before midnight." Bond sounded relieved, but the line had gone dead long before he took the handset from his ear.

"First hurdle." Holy jabbed down on the recorder's stop button. "Now, you have to be convincing when you get there."

"So far, it's playing to packed houses." Tamil Rahani sounded pleased. "And the dispatch rider brings the Frequency up from Cheltenham at around eleven-forty-five, yes?"

"If the President of the United States is away from his own country, yes." Bond held the man's eyes, trying to discern his state of mind.

Rahani laughed. "Oh, he's out of the country. No doubt about that, Commander Bond. No doubt at all."

"If you leave here at nine-forty-five you should make it with time to spare," Holy said, removing his headset. "We'll be with you all the way, James. All the way."

– 17 –

Down Escalator

THE METAL FORESTS of antennae that rise above the massive pile of government buildings, running from Downing Street along Whitehall and Parliament Street, conjure thoughts of communications flitting in through the night, of telephones ringing in darkened houses, wakening ministers, calling them to deal with important crises, of the fabled "telegrams" crossing the airwaves from distant embassies.

In fact, only clear, precise and open messages run into those government offices. Sensitive signals, and urgent information messages, are usually routed from the GCHQ complex outside Cheltenham, or one of its many satellites. From Cheltenham they pass through the mystery building known as Century

House, or to the Regent's Park Office. Ciphers, for the Foreign Office only, then go, not to Whitehall and Parliament Street, but to an unimposing, narrow, four-story house off Northumberland Avenue.

They are sent by a variety of methods, ranging from the humble dispatch rider to teleprinter by land-line; or even through a closed telephone circuit, often linked to a computer modem. Certainly there are plenty of dedicated computers in the house near Northumberland Avenue; dedicated, that is, to the art of quick deciphering.

If the romantically minded also imagined that someone with the title of Duty Security Officer, Foreign Office, prowls the great corridors of power with flashlight and uniformed accomplices, they would be wrong. The DSOFO does not prowl. He sits, in the house off Northumberland Avenue, and his security job is to ensure that all ciphers, for Foreign Office only, remain secure and get to the right person. He also deals with a mass of restricted information concerning communications from abroad, both from British sources and those of foreign powers. Leaders of friendly foreign powers, in particular, look for assistance from the Foreign Office. They usually find it with the DSOFO.

It was to the little-noticed turning off Northumberland Avenue that James Bond was now heading in the Mulsanne Turbo.

They had taken him out to the garage shortly

after nine-thirty, made sure he had money, credit cards, his ASP and petrol in the tank. Holy, Rahani and Zwingli had, in turn, shaken his hand and promptly at nine-forty-five, the Bentley eased onto the gravel turning circle, flashed lights once and swept on its stately way up the drive, onto the road toward Banbury.

From Banbury, Bond followed the route they had ordered him to take—straight to the M4 motorway, and so into London.

He did not spot any shadows. No doubt they were there, but the possibility caused him little concern. The street in which he would finally stop would have been well cleared of all but authorized vehicles, and, unless SPECTRE had someone with supernatural powers, there was little chance of his being observed once he'd entered the parking area.

Risking the wrath of police patrols, Bond made the journey at speed. From numerous telltale signs and bumps he was certain Peter Amadeus had managed to let himself into the car's boot. He could survive for long enough, but the little programer would, by now, be suffering great discomfort. He stopped once, at the service station near Heathrow Airport, to fill the tank. There he was able to let a little air into the boot and satisfy himself that Amadeus was, indeed, alive, well, and living in the Mulsanne. Whispering, he explained the impossibility of releasing his traveling companion—reassuring him that it would not be long now.

Less than forty minutes later, Amadeus was freed, speechless and stiff from the cramped, uncomfortable ride, but duly grateful.

"Well, this is where you show your gratitude," Bond said. He took the programer's arm firmly and led him toward the lighted doorway of the terraced house.

Swing doors opened onto a marble-tiled hallway with a lift that took them to the second floor and a minuscule landing watched over by a government guard, who half rose from his desk to ask what they required.

"Predator," Bond snapped at him. "Tell them, Predator and friend."

Less than a minute later, they were led quickly through a passage and into a larger room. The red velvet curtains were drawn, a portrait of the Queen hung over the Adam fireplace—there was another, of Winston Churchill, on one wall—while a long boardroom table gleaming like a wooden flight deck occupied a large portion of the available space.

Six faces turned as one. M, with Bill Tanner on his right, and another officer Bond recognized to the left: Major Boothroyd, the Armorer—Head of Q Section—sat to Tanner's right with Lady Freddie Fortune next to him.

Bond did not have time to be surprised at Freddie's presence, for the sixth member of the reception committee left her chair almost at a run.

"James, darling. Oh, it's so good to see you!" And Percy Proud, oblivious to the officialdom around her, held him close, as though she would never let go again.

"Commander Bond! Miss Proud!" M was genuinely embarrassed. "I, er, think we have important work to do."

Bond detached himself from Percy, acknowledged the others, and introduced Peter. "I think Dr. Amadeus will be able to contribute." He glanced often and suspiciously at Freddie Fortune, so often that M finally said, "Lady Freddie's been on the team for some years. Done good work. Sound woman, 007, very deep cover indeed. You are to forget you've ever seen her here."

Bond caught Freddie's steady gaze, returned it with a sardonic smile and cocked eyebrow. Then M drew the conference to order.

"I trust you've gone into Endor, sir . . ." Bond started.

"Yes, 007. Yes, we went in about an hour after you drove out, but the birds had flown. I don't think many could have been left there by the time you departed. They have vanished into thin air. Bag and baggage. We thought you could tell us . . ."

"I'm instructed to return there. By the same route as I came." He recalled the deserted feel of the place

that morning, and the fact that he had only seen
Cindy and the Arab, then Tigerbalm, Holy, Rahani
and Zwingli later on. "The cars were still there,
though." It sounded a lame comment, even as he said
it. "Three of them. Still in the garage."

"Two when our people arrived," the officer said,
the one Bond recognized but could not name.

"How about mine? How about Cindy?" Percy
touched his sleeve, and Bond could not meet her
eyes.

"I'm not certain. She was a great deal of help, last
night. Even tried to steal a copy of their main program—the simulation of whatever they're doing." He
turned to M. "It's on SPECTRE's instructions, this
business, sir. Did you know?"

"Is it indeed?" M could give the iceberg treatment
when he had a mind. "That villainous scum is on the
warpath again, eh?"

"You still haven't told me about Cindy?" Percy
had her hand tightly on his arm now.

"I just don't know, Percy. I've no idea." He told
her about the previous night, leaving out all that happened after he got back to her room but repeating
Holy's comments of the morning.

"So we have no ideas about this simulation?" M
sucked at his pipe.

"If I could have a word." They all turned toward
the forgotten man, Peter Amadeus. "I've seen the
simulation running. It was a couple of weeks ago. I

couldn't sleep. I went down to the laboratory in the middle of the night, and Jason was in what we call the War Room—Mr. Bond knows: It's at the far end. Jason was engrossed. Just didn't hear me," he passed a hand across his forehead. "That was before all those great oafs—the gun-happy boys—turned up. Before I got the vapors about being there."

M looked uncomfortable, sucking noisily at his pipe.

"Well, thinks I, have a look, Pete. See what the crooks are after next. They refer to it as The Balloon—"

"The Balloon Game, yes," Bond interrupted.

"I've seen it and you haven't. I have the floor, Mr. Bond, please." Peter Amadeus looked around him— a minuscule prima donna. "As I was saying, they all called it The Balloon Game, but it's to do with something they've named Operation Down Escalator."

M's brow creased as he repeated the words under his breath.

"The simulation," Amadeus raised his voice, "appears to be set in a commercial airport. Not large. I didn't recognize it, but that's nothing to go by. The scenario begins in an office complex just to the left of the main terminal building. There's a lot of stuff with cars and positioning men. As far as I could see, the idea was to lift one man."

"Lift?" From M.

"Kidnap, sir," Bond clarified.

Amadeus scowled at them, as though to say he didn't like being interrupted. "They lift this chap, and there's a lot of changing around in cars—you know, he's taken to one point, then switched to another car. Then the location alters. A smaller field—an airfield. Tiny, with a mini control tower and one main building, a hanger, and—guess what? An airship."

"Airship?" From Bond.

"Hence Balloon Game. They get onto this field using the man they've lifted. It does appear to be terribly clever—there are three cars, twelve men, and the hostage, if that's what he is. Result? They take over the whole shooting match. There is a final scenario, and that's to do with flying the airship to a certain point. It got very technical and—"

"Chief of Staff," M almost butted in. "Go and check it out. We know the thing's there, because it's on the itinerary. Saw it myself. They cleared it with the President's people, the Prime Minister, and the Russians. Doing a sort of fly-past tomorrow morning."

Bill Tanner was out of the room before he finished.

Bond looked at his chief, the questions clear on his face. "Sir, I haven't seen, or heard, any news since . . . They even immobilized the car radio . . . Could you?"

"Yes," M leaned back. "At least we've now got a small conception of what it's about. We know where, and how. What? Well, that's a very different matter."

256

"Sir," Bond prompted.

"It's been kept under wraps for some time—a good few months in fact," M began. "These things always take the devil of a time to organize, and the participants wanted it to remain very low profile. Tonight, members of a summit conference are to arrive in Geneva. In fact the first main session *is* this very night. They've taken over the whole of Le Richemond Hotel for three days . . ."

"Who, sir?"

"Russia, the United States of America, Great Britain, France and West Germany. The President of the United States; the French President; the Chairman of the USSR; the German Chancellor; our Prime Minister—with all advisers, secretaries, military, the entire circus. Aim? To come to a collective agreement regarding arms control, and to seek a more positive and prosperous future. The usual pie-in-the-sky impossibilities."

"The airship?" The more Bond heard, the less he liked it.

"Goodyear. They have their ship, *Europa,* in Switzerland at the moment. When they heard about the summit, Goodyear asked permission to fly what they called "a goodwill mission," taking them straight over Le Richemond. They've got the blimp tethered just up the lake, on a small strip—a tiny satellite field you can only approach from the lake itself. Mountain rescue boys and some private flyers use it."

257

"But when did Goodyear arrange this?" Bond had not heard a whisper about any summit conference.

M grunted. "You know what it's like, 007. They arrange their flights a year in advance. The *Europa* would have been there in any case. Would've been flying. However, they had to get permission once the conference was announced."

Percy, it seemed, had caught on. "Dr. Amadeus, when did you first hear about The Balloon Game?"

About four months ago, he told her. Four or five.

"And the Summit . . . ?"

"Has been penciled in for a year," M nodded. "Information available through diplomatic channels. The Press have been good boys for a change. Not a whisper, even though they must have known."

Bill Tanner returned with the news that he had been in contact with Geneva. "I talked to the Goodyear security man out at the strip. No problems, and we've alerted the Swiss police. They're going to close the field to everyone but accredited Goodyear staff. That means around thirty—thirty-five—people, handlers, publicity and PR, mechanics, two pilots. Nobody's going to get in unless the Goodyear representatives okay bona fides. Sewn up, sir."

"Right. Well, Bond, all we have to do now is sew up the remainder of this unpleasant lot. Any ideas?"

Bond had one idea, and one only. "You give me the EPOC Frequency, sir—the real one, just in case they already have it. Because I wouldn't put anything past SPECTRE and this crowd who're doing their dirty work for them."

"Oh, yes, the EPOC Frequency. That was mentioned in your message. Made us think. Tell me about that, 007."

He went through the essentials of the story, from start to finish, leaving out nothing. "They claimed to have the Russian equivalent, sir. And the Emergency ciphers for both Russia and the United States of America. I tend to believe them."

M nodded. "Yes, SPECTRE's never been backward in acquiring information. Good job we've got the Goodyear field under wraps, Chief of Staff. Chivvy the Swiss, would you; and keep in contact with the Goodyear people." He began to expand on his own theory.

If they did have the Emergency ciphers of the United States, and Russia, together with the frequencies, there was no theoretical reason why—if SPECTRE's agents could get very near to the leaders of the two superpowers—they should not activate any one of the Emergency ciphers.

"That means," Bond caught up with him, "they could hijack the airship, load enough shortwave hardware, plus a computer on board. Do the Goodyear goodwill flight, taking them right over the very spot where heads of state are gathered together . . ."

"That's it, Bond! Directly overhead would be enough for the United States' communications satellite to justify the cipher, and, I presume, the Russian one also."

It meant there were several possibilities. Full nuclear strikes by one or the other country, or a simultaneous strike by both, knocking out the superpowers in one preposterous cloud of death, with nothing but desolation on the two great continents for years to come. It was unthinkable. M said so, loudly. Bond, in turn, pointed out that Jay Autem Holy had talked only of peace. "There would be danger, but only in the event of my not returning with the EPOC Frequency."

"There's one alternative." M looked around the room, receiving no help from the faces gathered about the table. "Ploughshare," he said, as though this was the answer to everyone's dreams. "Ploughshare, and the Russian equivalent—whatever that is."

Percy asked what Ploughshare was, and M, with a rare smile, explained. A way, he said, of consigning all nuclear weapons—the bulk of them anyway—to the scrap heap. "The last great failsafe. The final hope." Quietly he told them of the one cipher that could be sent over the EPOC Frequency that would set in motion the destruction of all arming codes, and the disarming of all nuclear weapons—"strategic and tactical. It's been reckoned that the process will take around twenty-four hours, in the United States. I should imagine a little longer in the Soviet Union. Just as there's always been a Doomsday Machine, we've had a Swords-to-Ploughshares Machine for the last three decades.

"It's there in the event of some catastrophe—like a sixty-seventy percent paralysis of the armed forces; some disastrous nerve gas; or a genuine stalemate, a Mexican stand-off, where the only way out is for everyone to drop their guns, if you follow me. Of course it's always been hoped that, if the Ploughshare option was taken, it would be by mutual understanding. But it's there. And it's just as potentially dangerous as blowing two great nations to pieces, because what would be the easiest way of destabilizing the two superpowers? Remove their nuclear balance at a stroke. Do that, and the stage is set for real revolution, economic disaster, and survival of the fittest."

Yes, M continued, Bond was right. Let him be supplied with the EPOC Frequency, plus a homing device, one or two of the Armorer's more fancy pieces of equipment, and a good surveillance team in addition. "You can then go back from whence you came, 007. Somewhere along the way, they'll pick you up, and we'll track you—safe enough if the team stays well back."

They took him off into a side room, where Major Boothroyd wired three homing devices into his clothes, and one for luck into the heel of his right shoe. The Armorer then handed over a couple of other small weapons—"Just in case"—and they gave him five minutes with Percy.

She clung to him; kissed him; told him to take care. There would be time enough, once this was over. He said there was no doubt about it, and the haymaking season would last all summer. Percy smiled the knowing smile women the world over smile when they've got what they really want.

Back in the conference room, they gave him the EPOC Frequency that had come into effect at midnight. It was now one in the morning, and Bill Tanner gave the final hasty briefing.

"We've already got your homers on two scanners," he said. "Don't worry, James, they've a range of almost ten miles. The car behind will stay only a mile or so away. The one riding point is already on his way. We know the route, so as soon as you go astray, we'll be in action. One SAS team standing by. They'll be anywhere in a matter of minutes, in a straight line, as the chopper flies. Good luck."

Even the center of London was starting to slow down, and Bond had the Bentley on the Hammersmith Flyover, heading out toward the M4, in less than twelve minutes. He began to burn up the road, thinking—as they all thought—that Holy and Rahani wouldn't try anything until he was well along the motorway.

It happened just after the Heathrow Airport turn-off.

First, a pair of cars, traveling at great speed, forced the Bentley to give up the fast lane. Bond cursed them for a couple of fools and pulled into the middle lane.

Before he realized what was happening the two cars reduced speed, riding beside him, keeping him in the center, while two heavy goods lorries came up in the slow lane.

Bond increased speed, trying to slip away in the center, but both cars and lorries were well souped up, and—too late—he saw the way ahead was blocked by a big, slow-moving, slab-sided refrigerated truck.

He braked to hold back from the truck and, unbelieving at first, saw the rear doors open, and a ramp slide out, its rear end riding on buffered wheels, fishtailing to the road surface, the whole thing being driven with exceptional precision.

The cars to the right, the lorries on the left, crowded him like sheep dogs working together until he had no option left. With a slight jerk, the Bentley's front wheels touched the ramp. With the wheel bucking in his hands, Bond glided into the great white moving garage.

The doors clanged shut behind him. Lights came on, and his side door was opened. Simon stood beside the car, an Uzi tucked under one arm. "Well done, James. We couldn't give you any warning. Now, there's not much time. Out of those clothes—off with everything. We've brought the rest of your gear. Everything off, shoes as well, just in case they smelled a rat and bugged you."

Hands grasped at his clothing, tearing it from him, handing over other things—socks, underwear, gray slacks, white shirt, tie, blazer, and soft leather moccasins.

When he turned around, Simon was behind him, now dressed in a chauffeur's uniform, and the van seemed to have slowed down, taking one of the exits. The ASP was handed back to him—a sign of good faith? He wondered if it was loaded. Certainly the whole team had worked with such speed and proficiency that Bond hardly had time to take in what was going on.

As the truck shuddered to a halt, Simon opened the Bentley's rear door, half pushing Bond into the back, and in a second the truck's doors were again open, and they were reversing out. Simon, the chauffeur, driving; the Arab boy, who had served breakfast that morning—no, yesterday morning—next to him, and—

"Well done, James. You got the Frequency, I presume?" Jay Autem Holy said from beside him.

"Yes," his voice sounded numb.

"I knew it. Good. Give it to me now."

Bond parroted the figures, and the decimal point. "Where're we going?"

Holy repeated the Frequency, asking for confirmation, and by now they were moving smoothly back on to the motorway.

"Where are we going, James? Don't worry, we're

264

going to live through an important moment in history. First, Heathrow Airport. All the formalities have been taken care of. We are just a little late and we're cleared to drive straight up to the private jet. We're going to Switzerland. Be there in a couple of hours. Then another short journey. Then yet another kind of flight. You see—I shall explain it in detail later—yesterday morning, long before you woke for breakfast, while it was still dark, the team from Erewhon carried out a smooth, and very successful, raid. They stole a small landing strip, and an airship. In the morning, James, we're all going for an airship ride. To change history."

A mile or so back down the road, the trail car observer had noted that their target seemed to pull off the motorway for a few minutes. "We're closing on him. Can't make it out. You want me to call in?"

"Give it a minute," the driver shifted in his seat.

"Ah. No," the observer stared at the moving blip that was James Bond's homer. "No, it's okay. Looks as though they were right. He's on his way to Oxford. Lay you odds on them picking him up between Oxford and Banbury."

But the Bentley had, in fact, just passed them, going in the opposite direction, hurling itself back toward Heathrow and a waiting executive jet.

– 18 –

The Magic Carpet

THE EXECUTIVE JET had Goodyear symbols all over it: a smart livery, with the words *Good Year* flanking the winged sandal. It also had a British registration.

The realization that he was outnumbered and outgunned held Bond back from making a run for it. Whoever had really laid out the ground plan of the operation—Holy, Rahani, or the inner council of SPECTRE itself—had done so with exceptional attention to detail.

For all he knew, the whole gang on board could prove genuine affiliation to Goodyear. In any case he did not even know if the ASP was loaded, and—so far—there was at least a small residue of trust between him and the main protagonists. Exploit the trust to the full, he told himself, so he just went along for the ride.

After takeoff, an attractive girl served coffee. Bond then excused himself and went to the pocket-sized lavatory at the rear of the aircraft.

Simon sat near the door and eyed him with amused wariness. But there was no attempt at restraint.

Instead Bond took out the ASP and slipped the magazine from the butt. It was, as he had thought, empty. Whatever else happened, ammunition, or another weapon, was a top priority.

Back in his seat, Bond tried to work out a logical sequence of events. M and his staff, in London, were obviously unaware of the situation near Geneva. The takeover of the Goodyear base, together with the airship *Europa*, had already happened hours before Bill Tanner had checked. True, the Swiss police were now alerted, but they would only make SPECTRE's task more secure by keeping out unwanted meddlers.

The Goodyear man to whom Tanner had spoken would have been one of Holy's or Rahani's men. The only possibility of action being taken by his Service would come from the surveillance cars losing him, but heaven knew how long it would take for them to discover he was gone.

Not for the first time in his career, Bond was truly alone. On the face of it, there was very little he could do to stop the airship's scheduled flight over Geneva and the use of the Russian and United States EPOC ciphers. Even the high security classification of these ciphers would work against them. If M was correct, and the plan turned out to be the operation of the American Ploughshare cipher together with its Russian equivalent, there would be no worldwide alerts. And if the Russian and American leaders remained incommunicado, locked within their summit talks, the damage would already have been done by the time they learned of it.

Sitting next to Jay Autem Holy, Bond reflected on the ingenuity of the plan. The two superpowers almost denuded of their one great strength—their one true weapon in the power balance. It was, of course, what many people had dreamed of, protested for and argued over for years. M had stressed this at the meeting in the house off Northumberland Avenue. He had also underlined that an agreed reduction of stockpiled nuclear arms and a steady phasing out of these instruments of potential doom was one thing, but for the two superpowers to be suddenly stripped, overnight, would cause a collapse of the system that had allowed a certain calm and sanity, however precarious, to prevail over the globe since World War II.

M had gone on to say that any historian, or economist, could map out the events that would follow the undercutting of stability. First would come a financial panic and market crash of enormous proportions, for who would have confidence in the great nations once their most terrible power was gone? The United States and Russia would be at the mercy of any other nation—however small—that possessed its own nuclear capability: China, France, possibly Iraq, Iran, Libya, Argentina, Israel. As his mind reviewed the pictures that M had drawn, vividly describing what would happen in this new world, Bond became more determined. He had to stop Down Escalator from proceeding, no matter what the cost to himself; for if it succeeded, history would indeed be changed.

"Anarchy will rule," M had declaimed in a rare burst of almost Churchillian oratory. "The world, as we know it, will divide into uncertain alliances and the man in the street—no matter what his birthright, nationality or politics—will be forced to accept a way of life that will drop him, like a handful of sand, into a dark and bitter well of misery. Freedom, even the compromise freedom we now enjoy, will be erased from the dictionary of life."

"Seatbelt, James." Bond opened his eyes. He hadn't been asleep, only lost in thought, but Jay Autem Holy was shaking his shoulder. "We're coming in to land."

Bond glanced at his watch. It was not yet six in the morning, and out of the cabin window, as the aircraft banked on its final approach, the sky was beginning to brighten in a dark gray colorwash sprinkled with lights.

"Where are we landing?" In Geneva, he guessed? He knew the airport well. Maybe—just maybe—he could get away there and raise the alarm.

270

"Bern, Switzerland. You remember, don't you? We're flying into Switzerland?"

Bern. That meant an overland trip of some duration. It also meant he would have to bide his time.

"Nice place, Bern," he casually observed, and Holy nodded.

"We go on by car. An hour—hour and a half. There'll be plenty of time. What has to be done doesn't start until eleven."

They came in, engines throttled back, then a final short burst of power to lift them over the threshold, and hardly a bump as the wheels touched. They parked well away from the main terminal, and two Audi Quatros and a police car pulled up alongside.

From his window, Bond watched the transaction take place: the small pile of passports handed over, inspected and returned, with a brisk salute—a combination of Swiss efficiency and SPECTRE's cunning. There would be no customs inspection, he guessed. The Goodyear jet must have been running in and out of Switzerland for a month or more now. They would have the formalities cut down to the fine art of mutual trust.

By the time they left the aircraft, in single file, Bond hemmed in neatly by the Arab boy and Simon, the police car was already slowly disappearing toward the terminal building in the half light of dawn.

The Audis had Goodyear VIP stickers on the windshields and rear windows. Bond recognized both drivers, in their gray uniforms, as men he had spotted in Erewhon.

Within minutes, he was sitting next to Holy in the rear of the second car, and they swept away from the airport. Behind them, another plane started its engines. Most of the houses on Bern's outskirts still slept, while others appeared to be just waking—lights coming on, green shutters open. Always, in Switzerland, Bond thought, you knew you were in a small, rich country, for—however big—the houses, offices, churches and railways looked as though they had been assembled in some sterile room, from a plastic kit complete with small details of greenery and flowers.

They took the most direct route—straight to Lausanne, then along the lake road, following the line of the toylike railway.

Holy was quiet for most of the journey, but Simon, sitting in the front passenger seat, occasionally turned back to ask fatuous, insignificant questions—"You know this part of the world, James?" "Fairytale country, isn't it?"

Bond remembered, for no apparent reason, that he'd been sixteen the first time he had visited Lake Geneva. He had spent a week with friends in Montreux, had a small affair with a waitress from a lakeside café, and developed a taste for Campari–soda.

Between Lausanne and Morges they stopped at a lighted lakeside restaurant where Simon and the

Arab boy went, in turns, to bring coffee and rolls out to the cars. The sheer normality of their actions grated on Bond's nerves, like a probe on a raw tooth. Half of his mind and body urged him to take drastic action, now; the other, more professional, half told him to wait, and to seize the moment only when it came.

"Where're we actually heading?" he asked Holy, soon after the breakfast break.

"A few kilometers this side of Geneva." The Holy Terror remained relaxed, in perfect control of himself. "We turn off the lake road. There's a small valley and an airstrip. The team from Erewhon will be waiting for us. You ever flown in an airship, James?"

"No."

"Then it will be a new experience for us both. I'm told it's totally fantastic." He peered from the windows. "And it looks as though we'll have a clear day for it. The view should be wonderful."

They went through Nyon, where the houses clustered together as though to keep themselves from falling into the lake. Then, soon after, Geneva came into view at the western end, a misty blur of buildings, while a toy steamer, ploughing a lone furrow of spray, chugged across the water.

They also met their first police checkpoint. The cars slowed almost to a standstill before the sharp-eyed uniformed men waved them on.

There was a second police roadblock just before they turned inland. A car, two motorcycle cops.

273

These too started to flag them down, until they spotted the Goodyear stickers. Then they waved them through, and as Bond looked back, he saw one of the men talking into a radio. The police, he realized, were assisting, however innocently, in the events planned to take place over the lake in a few hours.

The great cleft in the mountains seemed to widen as the road climbed. The sun was up now, and up the slopes one could see tiny farmhouses, plateaus with animals grazing. Then, suddenly, the valley floor and the tiny landing strip appeared a little below them— the grass a painted green, the control tower, hangar and one building as neat, and unreal, as a movie set.

Out on the grass, two mountain rescue aircraft were parked like stranded birds, and at the far end of the field the sausage shape of the Goodyear airship *Europa* swung lazily, tethered to her low portable masthead.

Then the road dipped, the airfield disappeared, and they were twisting through the S-bends that would carry them to the final destination.

Before the two cars reached the airstrip, two more police checkpoints were negotiated. The Swiss police had certainly snapped into action. London, Bond decided, would feel very satisfied.

There were no less than three more police cars at the airstrip entrance, which was little more than a metal gateway set into an eight-foot chain-link fence, circling the entire strip. In the distance, a police car patrolled the perimeter, as slowly and thoroughly as only the Swiss perform their official duties.

The Audis drew up to the gate, and Bond saw two faces—again recognized from Erewhon. This time, though, the men were dressed in smart suits and smiled broadly as the two-vehicle convoy came to a halt. They exchanged a few words with the senior policeman on the gate, then climbed into the Audis, one to each car.

The man who entered Bond's car was a German, fair-haired, suspicious-looking, and with features cut from a solid block of rough stone. He appeared to be in his mid-twenties, and the smart suit bulged around the breast pocket. Bond did not like the look of him. He liked him even less when the talking started.

The two cars headed not for the little office building but for the hangar, where the two slab-winged Pilatus aircraft sat. Meanwhile, Holy confined himself to only the most pertinent questions, and was given precise, military answers, in an American-tinged accent.

Rudi—that was the German's name—had all the answers and then some. Posing as the Goodyear head of PR he had taken the call from Bill Tanner, which he now described in detail, saying the man was certainly English, and also undoubtedly represented one of the major British security agencies. The police—he said—began to arrive within half an hour of his call.

Jay Autem then asked about the timing. It didn't

take him long to deduce that the first call had come even while Bond was in the Foreign Office house off Northumberland Avenue.

"James," he said, turning to Bond, the great bird eyes narrowing. "How much did you tell your friend . . . uh, what was his name?"

"What friend?" Bond answered.

"Denton. Last night. Anthony Denton."

"Me?" Bond looked surprised and startled, as though he hadn't been paying attention to the conversation. "What *could* I have told him?"

Holy stared at him. "Don't be naive, James. Tamil's people took over this airstrip yesterday morning. Nobody suspected, there was no trouble. Not until last night, that is, when you were getting the EPOC Frequency for us. Why, I ask myself, should the Swiss police begin to take an interest in us at that time of night?"

Bond shrugged, indifferent. He had no idea, he said. In any case, whatever had happened had nothing to do with him.

The cars came to a halt. Holy shifted again in his seat.

"I do hope you've given us the correct frequency, James. If you haven't . . . Well, I've already warned you of the consequences. Consequences for the entire world, my friend . . ."

"You've got it," Bond snapped back. "That's the current EPOC Frequency. Have no doubt about that, Dr. Holy."

276

Holy winced at the sound of his true name. Then he leaned forward to open the door.

Bond saw a moment of opportunity. As the others got out, he was left briefly with the Arab boy, who watched him with alert bright eyes, a small Walther automatic clutched in his right hand. The safety, Bond noticed, was off, but he could, he calculated, take the Arab out.

As abruptly, the moment faded. Even as Simon, Holy and the German, Rudi, were joined by Rahani and Joe Zwingli in a little procession walking to the hangar, Bond now saw Rahani's men everywhere he looked. Spread out, half concealed by what cover they could find in the shadows of the hangar and the aircraft, with a full armament of automatic weapons.

A small door, inserted in the great sliding panels of the hangar, was opened, and the party stepped inside. About two minutes later, Simon came out, striding quickly to the car.

"Colonel Rahani wants you inside," he said. His manner had become one of indifference—that of a man who wants no involvement with anyone outside his own tight comradeship. Bond recognized the psychology. They had come, it seemed, to some cutoff point.

It could be, Bond thought, as they walked the few paces toward the hangar, that the end was now. They'd decided he'd talked, and they had no further use for him. Curtain time.

The little group stood just inside the small door, and it was Tamil Rahani who greeted him.

"Ah, Commander Bond. We thought you should see this." His hand came up to gesture toward the center of the hangar. "A part of your education in our methods."

About forty men sat, close together on the floor, held into a tight knot by three machine guns, tripod-mounted, each with a crew of four.

"These are the good men from Goodyear," he split the Good-year, as though making a joke. "They will remain here until our mission is completed. You should know about this. They will be quickly dispatched—all of them—if one person makes an attempt to break out. Or if anything else goes wrong.

"It is uncomfortable for them, I know," Rahani continued. "But if all goes well, they will be released unharmed. You will notice, of course, there is one lady. I believe you know her, Commander."

From the middle of the group, Cindy Chalmer gave Bond a wan smile, and Tamil Rahani lowered his voice: "Between ourselves, Commander Bond, I think the delightful Miss Chalmer has little chance of surviving. But we want no bloodshed as yet. Not even your blood. You see, it was the original intention that you should be put with this group of prisoners, once you'd fulfilled your mission. The representative from SPECTRE—who did not trust you from the start—is not at all happy with you now. However," his lips widened, not into a smile, but rather a straight thin slash across his face. "However, I think you can be of use in the airship. You can fly, yes? You have a pilot's license?"

Bond nodded, adding that he had no experience of airships.

"You'll only be the copilot. The one who sees to it that the pilot does as he's told. There'll be a certain poetic irony in it, if by any chance you *have* doubled on us, Commander Bond. Come!"

Back to the cars, and a swift drive over the few hundred yards to the office building.

Inside, around forty of Rahani's trained men from Erewhon were sitting around, smoking and drinking coffee. "Our handling team, Commander Bond. They have learned by simulation. At Erewhon. It was something we did not show you, but they are very necessary when we weigh out the airship before takeoff; and, to a greater extent, when we get back from our short excursion."

Only one man looked out of place, and he sat at a table just inside the door. He wore a navy-blue pilot's uniform, and his peaked cap lay on the table in front of him. One of Rahani's hoods sat opposite, well clear of the table, with an Uzi machine pistol ready to blow the man's stomach out should he make a fuss.

"You are our pilot, I presume?" Rahani smiled politely at the man, who looked at him coldly and said yes, he was a pilot, but that he wouldn't fly under duress.

"I think you will." Confident, and quite unmoved. "What do we call you?"

"You call me Captain," the pilot replied.

"No. We're all friends here. Informal." Then, with a commanding snap: "Your first name."

The pilot did not seem one to be intimidated, but he hesitated, then cocked his head on one side. "Okay, you can call me Nick."

"Right, Nick," Tamil Rahani carefully explained what was going to happen. Nick was to fly the airship, just as he would have under normal circumstances. Up to Geneva, along the lakefront. After that he would change course, cutting straight over Le Richemond Hotel. "You will stay over the hotel for approximately four minutes," Rahani expressed himself as an officer used to being obeyed. "Four minutes at the outside. No more. Nothing will happen. Nobody'll be hurt, as long as you do what you're told. After that, you bring the ship back here and land. You will leave unharmed."

"Damned if I'll do it."

"I think you will, Nick. For one thing, we have forty of your fellow employees in the hangar. Should anything go wrong, they will die, instantly. For another, if you don't fly it, someone else will. This gentleman here, for instance," he touched Bond's shoulder. "He's a pilot—without airship experience, true—and will do it if we give him enough encouragement. Our encouragement to you is that we kill you, now, if you don't agree."

"He means it, Nick," Bond interrupted.

"Thank you, Commander," said Rahani.

The pilot thought for a moment, then seemed to lose his resolve under Rahani's implacable stare.

"Okay. Okay, I'll fly the blimp."

"Good. Now I'll tell you what we have in store for Commander Bond. Like God, he is your copilot. You will tell him, now, about the differences in flying an aircraft and handling an airship. In turn we are going to give him one round of ammunition for his automatic pistol. One round only. He can only kill, or wound, one person with that, and there'll be five of us on board. Five, not counting Commander Bond and yourself. Bond, here, will do exactly as I tell him. If you try to be clever, I will tell him to kill you—which will leave him with no ammunition. If he does not kill you, Simon—or one of us—will do it for him, and force him to take over. If he still resists, then we'll kill him also, and another of us will fly the ship. Do you understand me?"

"Yes, I understand you."

"Well, Commander Bond will look after you, and we'll all have a pleasant trip—how long? Half an hour?"

"About that. Maybe three-quarters."

"Commander Bond, talk to your pilot. Learn from him. We have things to get on board the gondola."

Bond lowered his head, letting his lips come near to the pilot's ear as he sat down. "I'm working under duress too. Just do what I tell you. We have to stop them." Then, in a normal voice: "Okay, Nick, you'd better tell me about this ship."

The pilot looked up, puzzled for a moment, but Bond nodded encouragement, and he began to talk.

Around them, Rahani's men were carrying equipment out of the office. Among the hardware, Bond saw one shortwave transmitter—a powerful one, from the look of it—and a micro as well.

Bond listened attentively to the pilot's instructions. Flying the airship, he said, was more or less the same as handling an aircraft. "Yoke, rudder pedals, same flight instruments, throttles for the two little engines. Only difference is in trimming the blimp." He explained how the two ballonets—fore and aft within the helium-filled envelope—could be inflated with air, or have the air valved off. "It's more or less the same principle as a balloon, except, with the air-filled ballonets, you don't have to bleed off expensive gas. You just take on or dump air. The ballonets take care of the gas pressure, give you extra lift, or allow you to trim down, or up. The only tricky part is knowing when to dump the pressure as you come in to land, to give the ground crew a shot at the guy ropes. The rest is a piece of cake."

It was all technically straightforward. Nick had hardly finished when Simon came over, glancing at his watch. The office was almost deserted.

"You're both needed at the ship." Simon held up one round of 9mm ammunition, and Bond saw that it was one of his original Glaser slugs. "You get this when we're aboard," he said, his eyes showing no compassion. "Now let's get moving."

At the airship, Rahani's men had readied themselves to take up the strain on the forward guy ropes. The others were already aboard the curved gondola which hung from the great gleaming sausage of the ship.

Nick climbed up first, through the large door that took up a third of the gondola's right-hand side. Bond followed, Simon taking up the rear and pulling the door closed behind him.

Tamil Rahani sat next to Holy at the back of the gondola. In front of them, they had arranged the transmitter, linked to the computer. The Arab boy sat directly in front of Holy, General Zwingli across the narrow aisle from him. Bond went to the front, taking his place on Nick's right. Simon now hovered between them.

As soon as he was in his seat, Nick became the complete professional, showing Bond the instrumentation, and pointing out the valves for the ballonets.

"Whenever you're ready," Rahani called out. Nick proceeded through his preflight checks, then slid his window open to shout down to the man in command of the ground crew. "Okay," he called. "Tell your crew to stand by. I'm starting up, and I'll give you a thumbs-up when they have to take strain." To Bond, he said he would be starting the port engine first. Immediately afterward, the starboard would fire.

"We fill the ballonets and while they're filling, I'll release us from the mooring mast. The boys outside, if they've been trained correctly, will take the strain, dump the hard bags of ballast hanging from the gondola." He turned, grinning, "After that, I trim the ship, lift the nose and we'll see if they have the sense to let go of the ropes."

Reaching forward, Nick started both engines, one after another, very fast, and set the air valves to fill.

As Bond was watching, Simon leaned forward, felt inside his jacket and removed the ASP. There was a double click, as the one round went into the breech, then the weapon was handed back. "You kill him, if the colonel gives the order. Otherwise I shoot you first, straight through the head."

Bond did not even acknowledge. By now he was following everything that Nick was doing, opening the throttles, pulling the lever that moored them to the mast, monitoring the pressure.

The airship's nose tilted upward, and Nick waved to the ground crew as he gave the engines full throttle. The nose slid higher and there was a slight sense of buoyancy, then, very slowly, they moved forward and upward: rock-steady, no tremor or vibration as they climbed away from the field. It was like riding on a magic carpet.

– 19 –

Ploughshare

IN HIS TIME James Bond had either flown, or flown in, most types of aircraft—from the old Tiger Moth biplane to Phantom jets—yet never had he experienced anything like the *Europa*.

The morning was clear and sunny, and could have been specially cleaned and prepared, as one so often suspects the Swiss of doing.

With its two little engines humming like a swarm of hornets—the single-blade, wooden pusher airscrews blurring into twin disks—the fat silver ship emerged from the wide cleft in the mountains, over the road and railway lines, and climbed above the lake. At a thousand feet, gazing out at the spectacular view, Bond even forgot—for a few seconds—his most dangerous mission.

It was the stability of the ship that amazed him most—that, and the lack of any buffeting of the kind one would get at a thousand feet in a conventional aircraft, over this type of terrain. No wonder those who traveled on the great airships of the twenties and thirties had fallen in love with them.

The blimp dipped its nose, almost stood on it. It turned a full circle—fifteen hundred feet now—so they caught a glimpse of the entire lake: the mountain peaks rising, touched with snow against the light blue sky; Montreux in the distance, with the Château Chillon a miniature poking into the water; the French side of the lake and the town of Thonon, peaceful and inviting.

Then Nick eased the ship around, so the view was of Geneva, and they approached at a stately fifty miles an hour.

Bond slewed his mind back to the present. He turned to look at the rear of the gondola. Rahani and Jay Autem Holy, oblivious to the view, were hunched over the transmitter. They had removed some of the seat backs, leaving Bond a good view of the radio, and he saw that it was linked up to the micro with its built-in drive.

Holy appeared to be muttering to himself as he tuned to the frequency. Rahani watched him closely—like a warder, Bond thought, while Zwingli

half-turned in his seat to give advice. Both Simon and
the Arab boy stood guard. The boy never took his
eyes off the pilot and Bond, while Simon leaned
against the door, almost as though he was covering
his masters as well.

Below them, the lakeside of Geneva slid into view.
The airship slowed, stood on its nose and turned
gently.

"No playing around, Nick," Rahani called, warning. "Just do what you normally do. Then take her
straight over Le Richemond."

"I'm doing what I normally do," the pilot said la-
conically. "I'm doing it by the book."

"And what," Bond called back, "are we really
doing anyway? What is this caper that's supposed to
change history?"

Holy lifted his eyes toward the flight deck.

"We are about to put the stability of the world's
two most powerful nations to the test. Would you
believe that the ciphers that can be sent through the
emergency networks of both the American President
and the Russian Chairman include programs to deac-
tivate their main nuclear capabilities?"

"I'd believe anything." Bond didn't need to hear
any more. M was right. The intention was to send the
United States Ploughshare program, and its Russian
counterpart, into their respective satellites, and from
there into irreversible action.

"Well, that's precisely what we're going to do,

James," Holy went on, the messianic tone entering his voice. "An end to the nuclear menace. Peace in our time. Peace on our planet."

Peace at the point of a gun, Bond thought but did not say. He glanced again at the armed Arab. It was at this moment that he decided upon his best, indeed his only, option.

His whole adult life had been dedicated to his country; now he knew his own life would be forfeit. There was one Glaser slug in the ASP. With luck, in the confined gondola it would blow any one of the men in half—but only one: So what was the use of a human target? Kill one, then be killed. But if he chose the right time, and the Arab boy could be distracted, the one Glaser slug, placed accurately, would decimate the radio, and possibly the micro as well.

He would die, very quickly, after taking out the hardware, but, for Bond, this was nothing compared to the satisfaction of smashing SPECTRE's plans one last time. Maybe they would try again, but there were always others behind him, others like himself, and the Service had been alerted.

The clean, ordered, picturesque Micropolis of Europe now lay to their right, as Nick gently turned the ship. Mont Blanc towered away above them. They began to descend to a thousand feet for his pass along the lakeside.

"How long?" It was the first time General Zwingli had spoken.

Nick glanced back. "To Le Richemond? Four minutes or so."

"You locked into that Frequency?" The old general now addressed Holy.

"We're on the Frequency, Joe. I've put the disk in. All we have to do is press the Enter key, and we'll know if Bond has been true to his word."

"You're activating the States first, then?"

"Yes, Joe." Rahani replied this time. "Yes, the United States of America get their instructions in a couple of minutes." He craned forward to look from the window. "Yes, there it is, coming up now."

Bond slid the safety off the ASP.

"Ready, Jay. Any minute." Rahani did not shout, yet the words carried clearly over the length of the gondola.

The luxurious hotel—a jewel among Geneva's resting places—was coming up below them. Nick held the blimp on a true course that would take them straight over the palatial building and its perfect gardens.

"I said ready, Jay."

"Any second. Okay," Holy answered.

At that precise moment, Bond, gripping the ASP, turned toward the Arab boy, shouting, "Your window! Look to your window!"

The Arab turned his head slightly, and Bond's hand came up, his brain telling him he had one chance, and one chance only.

He squeezed the trigger, and over the whirling engine noise, the solid clunk of the pistol's firing mechanism echoed through his ears.

For a second he could not believe it. A misfire? A dud round? Then came the laugh from Simon, echoed with a grunt from the Arab boy.

"Don't think of throwing it, James. I'll cut you down with one hand. You didn't honestly think we'd let you on board with a loaded gun, did you?"

"Damn you, Bond." Rahani was half out of his seat. "No gunplay—not in here. Have you given us the Frequency, or is that as false as your own treachery?"

The bleep and whir, from the back of the gondola, indicated that Holy had activated the cipher program. Now, he gave a whoop of joy: "It's okay, Tamil! Whatever else Bond's tried, he *has* given us the Frequency. It's been justified. The satellite's accepted it!"

Bond dropped the pistol, now a useless piece of metal. He had blown it. They had done it. At this moment, the massive machines in the Pentagon—or wherever they were located—would be sorting the numbers at that unbelievable rate of speed with which computers perform huge mathematical tasks. The instructions would be pouring out to similar machines, the length and breadth of the country—even to Europe and the NATO forces.

Now it was done. He felt only a terrible anger, and a sickness deep in his stomach.

What happened in the next few seconds took time to sink in. Holy was still whooping as he half rose, stretching out a hand, fingers snapping, toward Rahani. "Tamil, come on, the Russian program. You have it. I've locked onto their Frequency . . ." His voice rose with urgency. "Tamil!" Now shouting, "Tamil! The Russian program. Quickly."

Rahani gave a great bellowing laugh. "Come on, yourself, Jay. You didn't think we were really going to allow Russia to suffer the indignity of being stripped of her assets as well?"

Jay Autem Holy's mouth opened and closed, fish-like. "Wha . . . ? Wha . . . ? What d'you mean, Tamil? What . . . ?"

"Watch them!" Rahani snapped, and both Simon and the Arab boy appeared to stiffen to his command. "You can begin the return journey, Nick." Rahani spoke so quietly that Bond was amazed he could be heard above the steady motor buzz. "Look at the reality, Jay. Face the reality. Long ago, I took over as the chief executive of SPECTRE. Now we have done what we set out to do. I even gambled on your pawn, Bond, actually getting the EPOC Frequency to lead us on. Down Escalator was always simply intended to deal with the imperialistic power of the United States, which we should now be able to hand on a plate to our friends in the Soviet Union. You were only brought in to provide the training programs. We have no use for emotionally motivated fools like Zwingli and yourself. Do you understand me now?"

Jay Autem Holy let out a long and desperate keen, echoed only by General Zwingli's roar of anger.

"You bastard!" Zwingli started to move. "I wanted my country strong again, by putting both Russia and the United States on the same footing. You've sold out—You . . . !" Whereupon he launched himself at Rahani.

The Arab boy shot him. Once. Fast and accurate. One bullet split the old general's skull. He toppled over without a sound, and as the blast of the boy's weapon echoed in the confined space, a long bell-like boom, Jay Autem Holy leaped toward Rahani, arms outstretched to claw at his throat, the scream of his voice turning to a banshee wail of hate.

Rahani, with no room to back off, shot him in midspring, two rounds from a small hand gun Bond had not even noticed. But Holy's powerful leap, goaded by fury, carried his body on, so that he crashed, lifeless, on top of SPECTRE's leader, the man who had inherited the throne of the Blofeld family.

"Get us down!" Bond shouted at the pilot, Nick. "Just get us down!" In the confusion, he propelled himself toward the nearest target—Simon, who, his back to the flight deck, had taken a pace toward the tangle of bodies piled on the seats. Bond landed hard on Simon's back, one arm locking around his neck, the other delivering a mighty chopping blow that connected a fraction below the right ear.

Three things happened simultaneously. Off balance, Simon's weight shifted to the left just before Bond's blow landed. His hand, scrabbling for some kind of hold, hit the gondola door's locking device and the door swung open, bringing an urgent draft of air into the gondola. Second, as Simon went limp from the blow, the Arab boy fired at Bond, a fraction of a second late, for the bullet hit Simon's chest, making it a moot point as to how he died—whether from Bond's death chop or the Arab's bullet.

Whichever way he died, Simon's long military training produced a final reflex action. At the moment of his death, a great power seemed to force itself through his muscles. He broke free from Bond's grasp, turned and with a deathly grip on the Uzi machine pistol, fired half a burst of fire, rap, rap, rap, that cut the Arab almost in two.

Simon did not let go of the gun, not even then. He collapsed backward. No sound came from his throat. Simon simply fell through the gondola door, through a thousand feet of air until he reached his grave in the lake water below.

Bond made to grab at the Arab's Walther, now lying on the floor. He felt the sting of a bullet cutting a shallow furrow along the flesh above his right hip, and another sing past his ear.

His hand reached the Walther, feet slipping on the floor. But, as he turned, instinctively, toward where Tamil Rahani should be, finger taking up the pressure on the trigger, he realized the instigator of their whole drama was already gone.

"Parachute," Nick said clamly. "Little bastard had a parachute. Taken the dive."

Bond took a pace toward the gondola door, hanging on to the grab rail, and leaned out.

There, below, against the blue-gray water of the lake, was the white shape of Rahani's parachute, a light breeze carrying him away from Geneva toward the French side of the lake.

"Bound to pick him up," Bond said aloud.

"Could you close the door, please?" Nick's voice, calm as only an experienced pilot can sound under stress. "I've got to find somewhere to drop this blimp in." He switched on the flight radio, flicking the dial with finger and thumb, adjusting the headset he had not worn throughout the flight of disaster.

A few seconds later, he turned his head slightly as Bond slumped into the seat beside him. "We can go back to the strip. Apparently the Swiss military cleared it soon after we left. Looks as if we've had guardian angels watching over us."

They sat together around the balcony of M's room in the lakeside hotel. Bill Tanner, M himself, Cindy Chalmer, Percy and Bond, whose side still stung from the long bullet burn.

"You mean," Bond said, with cold anger, "that you already knew they had taken over the airstrip? You *knew* when you sent me off from London."

M nodded. He had recounted how—because of the tight security surrounding the summit conference—many interested parties had been given cipher words by which they could prove their authenticity by radio or telephone. On the night Bond had visited the Communications house off Northumberland Avenue, Bill Tanner's call to the Goodyear people had not elicited the correct sequence of identification.

"Therefore we knew something had gone wrong." M did not appear to be in the least bit concerned. "We alerted everyone with need to know; arranged with both the United States and the Soviet Union that any messages on their current emergency satellite frequencies should be accepted, but then stopped."

"I was to be thrown to the wolves, then," Bond retorted. "It wasn't necessary to the operation that I should be left in outer darkness, as you once so neatly put it. But you let me go, knowing full well . . ."

"Come, come," M put in tartly. Suddenly he leaned forward and placed a hand gently on Bond's arm. "It was for your own good as much as ours, James. After all, you might have found a way of bringing in Holy—or Rahani, come to that. But that wasn't uppermost in our minds. We had to find a way of restoring your good name. Look on it as a sort of rehabilitation."

"Rehabilitation?"

"You see," M went on quietly, "there had to be some role you could play for the sake of your public image. The Press aren't going to fail to notice hijinks on an airship overhead while the summit talks were going on. Geneva's been stiff with journalists these past few days. We told the Swiss authorities they could let a certain amount of reporting go through. Saves us a tricky hushing-up job in a way. I think you'll be pleased with what the papers say tomorrow."

Bond was silent. He gazed at M, who gave his arm a couple of reassuring pats.

"I suppose you'll want to take some sick leave because of that scratch," M said distantly.

Bond and Percy exchanged looks. "If it wouldn't inconvenience the Service, sir."

"A month, then? Let all this fuss die down. We can't have the whole department going public for the sake of your honor, 007."

Cindy spoke for the first time. "What about Dazzle? Mrs. St. John-Finnes?"

Tanner told them there had been no trace of the lady who called herself Dazzle, just as Rahani had disappeared into thin air. "A launch picked up his chute. He had drifted well inshore, on the French side."

"Damn. I wanted a little time alone with that bastard." The delightful Cindy Chalmer could be lethal when roused.

Percy gave her a wicked smile. "You, Cindy, are going straight back to Langley. The order came through this morning."

Cindy pouted, and Bond tried hard not to catch her eye. "And what about Dr. Amadeus?" he asked.

"Oh, we're taking care of him," Bill Tanner answered. "We've always room for good computer men in the Service. Anyway, Dr. Amadeus turned out to be a brave young man."

"There is something else," M grunted. "The Chief of Staff did not know this, but in checking back through the files when you alerted us to Rahani, 007, we found some interesting information. You recall we've been keeping surveillance on him for some time?"

Bond nodded as M slid a matte black-and-white print from the folder on his lap.

"Interesting?"

The photograph showed Tamil Rahani locked in an embrace with Dazzle St. John-Finnes. "Looks as though they had plans for the future."

Bond asked about Erewhon and was told that the Israelis had pinpointed the site.

"Nobody there. Deserted. But they're keeping an eye on it. I doubt if Rahani will visit it again. But he'll probably show up somewhere."

"Yes." Bond's voice was flat. "Yes, I don't think we've heard the last of him, sir. After all, he boasted that he was Blofeld's successor."

"Come to think of it," M mused. "I wonder if you should forgo that leave, 007. It may be vital to follow up . . ."

"He's got to rest, sir." Percy was almost ordering M. "For a short time at least." The Head of Service looked at the willowy ash-blonde, astonishment on his face.

"Yes. Yes. Well, if you put it like that . . . I suppose . . . yes."

– 20 –

End of the Affair

THEY FIRST FLEW TO ROME, for a week at the Villa Medici. Percy had never been to Rome, and James showed her almost everything one can see in seven short days.

From Rome they moved to Athens, and from Athens the couple traveled light on an island-hopping tour. First, the Aegean, then, doubling back, to the Ionian Sea, where they managed to find some secluded beaches, and tavernas, off the package deal routes.

It was a time of distant voices from the past. They told each other long tales of their youth, made their separate confessions, and became totally immersed in each other's bodies. For Percy and Bond, the world became young again, and time stood still, as only time can within the dark, secret mysteries of the Greek islands.

They ate lobster fresh from the sea, and Greek salads, and drank their fill of retsina. Sometimes the evenings ended with them dancing with the waiters, under the vines of a roadside taverna, doing all the arm-stretching, calf-slapping, and graceful swaying that goes with it. They discovered, as many have before, that the taverna owners of the islands know, and recognize, the signs of love and take lovers into their hearts.

All along—out of habit perhaps, for Percy was a lady of the same trade, but also out of some sixth sense—they kept a wary eye on strangers. They did not, though, spot a familiar face. Vehicles, even motorcycles, did not show twice. They were free, or so it seemed.

But SPECTRE's teams were numerous, and clever. Neither James Bond, nor Percy Proud, could know or see the shadows closing in around them.

The teams were usually five-handed, and they changed daily, never using the same car twice, always having a man or woman ready to follow on to the next island. A girl here, a happy Greek boy there; first a student, then a middle-aged English couple; old VWs, brand-new Hondas, middlebrow Peugeots. The leader's orders were clear, and, when the right moment came, he also arrived.

Bond and Percy spoke much of the future, but by the last week, while heading for Corfu—for they had decided they would fly to London direct from that island of cricket and ginger beer—they could still not come to any sure conclusion. They found a small bungalow of a hotel, away from the razzmatazz of the beehive modern glass and concrete palaces. It was close to a secluded beach, which could only be reached by clambering over rocks, and to a taverna. Their room looked out on a slope of dusty olive trees, and oddly Victorian-looking scrub.

In the late afternoon of each day, they would return to their room, and, as dusk closed in and the cicadas began their endless song, the couple would make love—long and tender, with a rewarding fulfillment of a kind that neither remembered experiencing before.

On their last night, with the small packing yet to be done and a special dinner ordered at the taverna, they followed their usual pattern, walking hand in hand up the slope, entering their room from the scrubby olive grove, leaving the windows open and the blinds drawn.

They soon became lost in each other, murmuring the sweet words of intimacy, enjoying their private island of physical pleasure.

They were hardly aware of the darkness, or the song of the night closing from the cicadas. Neither of them heard Tamil Rahani's car pull up quietly on the road below the hotel, for the heir to SPECTRE had chosen to be in at their death. Nor were they aware of his emissary, who moved up from the road sure-footed in rope-soled sandals, treading softly through the olives until he reached the window.

Tamil Rahani, the true and rightful successor to the Blofelds, had decreed they should both die. His one regret was that it would be quick.

The short, sallow-faced man, who was the best of SPECTRE's silent killers, peered through the lattice of the blinds, smiled, and carefully withdrew a six-inch ivory blowpipe. With even greater care he loaded the tiny, sharp wax dart—filled with deadly pure nicotine—and began to slide the end of the pipe through the lattice.

Percy lay, eyes closed, nearest the window. Her reaction was conceived in long training—for she was like an animal in her instinct for danger.

With a sudden move, she slid from under a startled Bond, one hand going for the floor and the small revolver that always lay at her side of the bed.

She fired twice, rolling naked on the floor as she did so—a textbook kill, for the man clearly outlined through the blinds was lifted back, as though in slow motion, his dying breath expelling the wax dart into the air.

Bond was beside her in a second, the ASP in his hand, and, as they emerged into the night air, both heard the sound of Rahani's car on the road below the hotel. They needed no superiors to tell them who it was.

Later, when the body had been removed, calls made to London and Washington, the police and other authorities satisfied, Bond and Percy drove into Corfu itself, to spend the night in one of the larger hotels.

"Well, at least that settles it. We should both know, now," Percy began.

"Know?" They had managed to get a meal of sorts in their room, though Bond found it hard to relax.

"The future, James. We should both know about the future after this episode."

"You mean that until Blofeld's successor is dead, neither of us will have peace?"

"That's part of it. Not all though." She paused to sip her wine. "I killed, James, automatically and . . ."

"And most efficiently, darling."

"Yes, that's what I mean. We're not like other people, are we? We're trained, and readied, and we obey orders—fly into danger at a moment's notice."

Bond thought for a moment. "You're right, of course, darling. What you mean is that people like us can't just stop, or live normal lives."

"That's it, my dear James. It's been the best time. The very best. But . . ."

"But now it's over?"

She nodded, and he leaned across the table to kiss

her. "Who knows?" Bond asked of nobody in particular.

The next morning they rebooked tickets, and Bond saw her off, watching her aircraft climb over the little hillock at the end of the runway, then turning to set course for the west.

In an hour, he would be on his way, back to London and one of his other lives, to play some other role for his country.

Bond went into the airport bar to wait for his flight to be called, passing the time with a large brandy, and musing on time past, and future. Percy had been right. It had been the best of times with her, but now his work called, and James Bond knew it would forever entice him back to new dangers—and new sweetness.